A TALE OF HELL
& OTHER WORKS
OF HORROR

A Tale of Hell & Other Works of Horror

STORIES OF WIZARDS, WEREWOLVES, SERIAL KILLERS, ALIEN WORLDS, AND THE DAMNED

Phil Slattery

Author

Slattery Publishing

Contents

I dedicate this book to my wife,
Francene Glynell Burnett Kilgore
Sanchez, who has been there for me
since the day we met.

First IngramSpark Printing, 2020

All stories in this collection are works of fiction. Any resemblance to actual people or organizations or events is coincidental and unintended.

This work contains adult language and situations. It may not be suitable for persons under the age of 18 years.

"Wolfsheim" was first published in *Midnight Times*, 2005.

"A Tale of Hell" was first published in *Midnight Times*, 2006.

"Dream Warrior" was first published in *Sorcerous Signals*, 2013

Murder by Plastic" was first published in Everyday Fiction, March 24, 2013.

"Shapeshifter" was first published in *Ascent Magazine* (www.ascentaspirations.ca) in 2003.

"Ivan" was first published in *Infernal Ink* in Volume 5, Issue 2, April 2016

"Sorcerer" was first published in *Creepy Campfire Quarterly* Issue #3, July 20, 2016

The other stories contained in *A Tale of Hell and Other Works of Horror* are being published for the first time.

"The mind is its own place, and in itself can make a heaven of hell, a hell of heaven."
~John Milton, *Paradise Lost*.

1

Preface

These are most of the short stories of the horror genre that I have had published to date. More can be found by scouring the Internet, but I do not consider those to be of the caliber of the ones contained here.

The inspiration for these came from a variety of sources. Sometimes, a place has a unique mood or feeling about it that I want to capture it in words. Sometimes a question or re-mark spurs something in the back of my mind that pesters me until I write it down.

Right now, as I sit at my dining table typing this, my neighbor in the duplex unit next to mine has apparently bought some puppies, who are howling in loneliness as their owner has left for a while. Coming through the concrete block walls, their long, plaintive howls remind me of the moaning of ghosts in old movies. I can imagine someone, perhaps a ghost hunter, walking, terrified, through the halls of an abandoned asylum, listening to these moans and quak-ing, his legs trembling, his eyes darting about, but for some reason he must push on deeper into the dilapidated bowels of the institute. At some point (not yet the end of the story), he finds the howls come from puppies someone has abandoned in the furnace room and whose cries echo through the ductwork. Who has abandoned them and why? Now one mystery has evolved into something more ominous and sinister. Is our protagonist alone in the building?

I hope you enjoy what follows.

2

A Tale of Hell

The last face Jack saw was the executioner's as he slid the needle into Jack's arm.

"I didn't mean to kill him," said Jack.

"The jury decided that you did," replied the executioner.

What seemed like several minutes passed while Jack, strapped to the gurney, sweated and waited, head throbbing with tension, watching the buzzing fluorescent lights overhead, until a black fog enveloped him.

He awoke standing naked holding two buckets overflowing with concentrated sewage. Sweat mixed with grime and soot rolled down his arms. The atmosphere, a mixture of steam, tear gas, sulfur, and the smell of death, burned his throat and stung his eyes filling them with tears. What little he could see glowed mottled orange and red. Thousands of naked men and women, covered in grime and sweat, cringed whimpering among jagged rocks or ran about in terror while lugging buckets of sewage, blood, or God knew what else.

A whip cracked across Jack's back. "Move your ass!" came a shout out of nowhere. Jack ran headlong with the buckets down a road of broken rock shoving his way through the throng. He stumbled and fell. The buckets spilled. The whip cracked. Jack tried to rise but the whip cracked again and drove him into the rock. "Move your ass! Move your ass!" Jack saw no one barking the order or wielding the whip, but the voice hurt his ears and the whip stung his face and shoulders. A trickle of blood ran down his chest. Jack leapt up and bounded over the rocks, buckets in hand, for several hundred yards.

Jack stumbled and fell again, scraping his knees and stomach. He gasped for air as he wiped the sweat and blood from his eyes. He could see that three more steps and he would have fallen over a cliff to drop twenty feet into a sea of lava. He dumped the few drops remaining in the buckets into the glowing surf. As Jack raised his face toward the horizon, he saw countless screaming men immersed to varying depths in the burning sea, some to their knees, some to their waists, some to their chins. In a few places he saw only arms whipping about above the surface.

A raw-boned man with wild eyes and a shaggy beard ran up to the edge and emptied his buckets into the lake.

"What is this place?" Jack shouted above the cacophony of hissing surf and the screams and wails of the damned.

"I don't know its name, don't know its name. No, don't know its name. It's where they send tyrants who sacrificed their nations for greed and power. They're all there. Yes, they're all there." The man scratched wildly at his arms and legs.

"I'm no tyrant."

"If you were, you'd be in there. Yes, you would. Yes, you would. What did you do?"

"I killed some damned bartender, just same damned moron! Now I have to rot in hell!"

"Ah, nothing special. You're just a slave, just a slave. Many souls come here for many crimes, some bad, some worse. The worse your crime, the worse your punishment. The worse. The worse." He continued scratching and nodding and then he giggled. "You're the damned moron. Yes, you are. You're the one who's damned!"

A thin, middle-eastern man with a wheelbarrow full of what seemed to be pale leather ran up, dumped it into the lake, then ran off.

"What was that?"

"Serial killers. Yes, serial killers. They're flayed every day and at night the skin grows back. Very nasty. Nasty. Nasty." The man now started clawing at his face.

Jack could see a bit better. The air was filled with drifting columns of oily smoke. Instead of a sky were countless stalactites. Millions of naked men and women carried buckets on stone causeways crisscrossing the glowing sea. Jack and the man stared at each other for a moment while others pushed through and unloaded. Jack glanced around. "Why aren't they beating us?"

The man switched back to scratching. "It's the game, s'th' game. They fuck fuck fuck with your mind as well as your body. Yes, they do."

Jack began to weep. "I'm going mad."

"No. No. No." The man laughed. "Madness is escape. They won't allow it. You'll never escape. You'll simply pick up a few quirks like I have, like I have, like I have, but your mind will always be sharp as a tack. That's the healing power of hell."

"How long have you been here?"

"Who knows? The last thing I remember was I was with Pickett's division at Gettysburg. We were storming the Yankee lines on top of a hill. Grapeshot was tearing our lines apart. Grapeshot. Grapeshot. Grapeshot!"

"Who are you?"

The man started clawing again. "No. No names. They want that. They want that. If you know someone's name, you'll become friends. Then when he's hurt, you'll sympathize and you'll hurt. Your suffering and pain will increase. Oh, it'll increase." He leaned his head straight back, looked at the ceiling, and closed his eyes, grimacing. "It'll increase. It'll increase. It'll increase."

Whips cracked across their backs. They raced back down the road, stumbling, cursing, almost veering off the causeway and into the lake.

Jack ran for what seemed miles, an invisible whip snapping on his skin every time he slowed, until he came to a long line of the damned, waiting to dip their buckets in a hot spring of sewage. Invisible whips lashed their backs while invisible demons barked out the single mindless command, "Move your ass! Move your ass!" Pushing forward, Jack became locked deep in the crushing grip of the crazed mob crowding to fill their buckets at the spring. He was thrown down onto his stomach into the edge of the boiling filth with a dozen others of the whimpering damned. Jack screamed and writhed and swept his buckets through the spring as he fought to the top of the slithering and clawing mass before being unexpectedly shoved out of the throng and into the open with his buckets less than half full just as a whip cracked across his back. Jack lurched forward into a run not knowing where to go, knowing only to run as long as he felt the lash of whips. When the whips stopped, he emptied his buckets into the nearest edge of the lake. When they cracked he fought his way through the mob to reach the nearest spring. He ran back to the line, fought his way through, filled his buckets, and raced back. A trickle flowed out. Again and again he repeated the mindless process until he finally turned and shouted into the black void overhead, "Fuck you! Fuck you! I'm not going to play your game! What more can you do to me? Fuck you!"

Jack flailed about with his arms trying to punch invisible demons and smashed into something soft and warm to his right that let out a wild yell.

Suddenly the darkness fell and Jack bolted upright in his own bed. It was daylight, he was covered with sweat, and his girlfriend was shaking his arm, shouting, "Jack! You're having a nightmare! Wake up! Wake up!"

Jack looked around. The sweat dripped off his forehead. He turned and saw Theresa staring at him with a bloody nose. Tears flooded her eyes. Jack couldn't catch his breath and lay back into his pillow gasping. Theresa smacked him across the face and began pounding with both fists, "You bastard! What are doing punching me while I'm asleep? You bastard!"

Jack held up his hands to cover his face, "I'm sorry, honey. I didn't mean to."

"What the hell's wrong with you?"

"I'm sorry already. I was having a nightmare. I didn't know what I was doing."

Theresa grabbed a Kleenex from the nightstand, held it to her nose, and tilted her head back. "What were you dreaming?"

"It was some weird-ass dream about carrying buckets of shit through hell."

"Well, if anyone ever deserved to tote shit through hell it's you. They've got the right man for that job."

"Aw, c'mon, honey. How can they send a sweetheart like me to hell?"

"Because of your temper, Jack. Your temper gets out of control."

"Shit, honey, I said I'm sorry. What more can I do?"

"You can pay my doctor's bill, that's what you can do, you bastard."

"I don't think we'll have to do that, honey. It's just a nosebleed."

"Nosebleed, my ass. It feels like it's broken. You're paying for my trip to the emergency room, you cheap bastard. If I have to have cosmetic surgery, you are paying for it too."

"The hell I will. It was an accident."

"It was your fault. You are paying."

"Honey, I haven't got the money right now. I'm up to my ears in debt."

"Bullshit, Jack. You spent over a hundred bucks on dinner and a concert last night. You're paying."

Jack was afraid that if he didn't pay for her nose job, he might lose her. They had fought before, and she had threatened to leave before, but she had never walked out. However,

Jack had never seen her beside herself with rage as she was then. This time, he thought, she might do it. If she did leave him, they wouldn't marry, and he would lose her inheritance and the connections that came with being part of her family. "I'm sorry, honey. You're right as always. I'll pay your bills. But first just lay back and let's see if it feels better in a little while. We might not even need a doctor."

After an hour, the bleeding stopped, but Theresa's nose was still sore and red. Jack placed an icepack on it and made some coffee while they waited to see if the swelling would go down. Jack was still trying to find a way to grovel sufficiently to please Theresa. "Tell you what, honey, let me fix you breakfast."

"You've never fixed breakfast for me before. What's up? You couldn't beat me to death in my sleep, so now you're going to poison me?"

Jack spoke firmly, the anger in him slowly rising. "I never laid a hand on you, woman, though it's not like I haven't been tempted."

Theresa's eyes narrowed as she fixed them unblinking on Jack's. She looked as if she were bracing to be slapped.

"I'm sorry. Let me calm down. I didn't mean that; I would never hit you. I honestly feel bad about bloodying your nose and I wish you would believe me. All I ask is that you let me make it up to you."

"Well, then fix me lunch, because it's almost noon."

Biting his tongue to prevent worsening the situation, Jack pulled on his jeans and a t-shirt and headed for the kitchen. His started to fix her favorite, a BLT, but when he turned on the gas burner, the blue flame and the whiff of burning gas brought out visions of thousands of emaciated men running helter-skelter screaming across the lava-filled seas of the underworld as invisible demons waded among them cracking invisible whips that ripped flesh like wet paper. Jack stood transfixed for a moment, sweating and gasping for air, engulfed in the vision, and then suddenly woke and remembered where he was. He turned off the burner, put the bacon back into the refrigerator, and took out the pimento cheese, bread, and materials for two garden salads.

When lunch was ready he set the table and called Theresa. They ate in silence with Theresa, still nursing her anger as well as her nose, seldom saying anything to Jack other than to pass the salad dressing, and Jack halfheartedly trying to placate her. When they finished, Jack put the leftovers in the refrigerator and put the dishes in the dishwasher. Theresa read the newspaper while holding a compress to her nose. Jack got an ashtray, book of matches, and a pack of cigarettes from the living room and, as he opened the pack, sat wondering what else he could do to help her get over her anger. He put a cigarette in his mouth and struck a match. The erupting match head startled him as he thought he saw a miniature man writhing in its flame. Theresa noticed Jack suddenly grimace and twitch, but said nothing and went back to her paper. Jack felt a cold sweat break out on his forehead, watched the flame for a second until the vision disappeared, then lit the cigarette and quickly blew out the flame.

For a couple of minutes they sat in silence, she nursing her nose, he smoking and concentrating upon a sunbeam that streamed across the table in a beautifully warm, yellow, diagonal line. It seemed as if there was an incredible amount of gentleness and softness in its very nature. He was fascinated not only by the sunbeam, but also by the fact that he had never noticed one this beautiful before. He couldn't understand the change that made this possible. How could he have gone his entire life without noticing this miracle of nature? Light, which had no substance to speak of and born in the sun among an infinite sea of nuclear detonations, any one of which could have swallowed this world, hurtled across time and space at a rate barely conceivable by the greatest minds on this planet, penetrated our atmosphere and ended in a gentle nuance that brightened his spirit and felt as warm and loving as a mother's caress on his skin. Now it seemed so blatantly obvious, he felt as if he had been a fool for his entire existence. Jack finished the cigarette and tossed it into the ashtray. "How's the nose, honey? Is it feeling better yet?"

Theresa sniffled. "A little. But I'm still not forgiving you just yet."

"Would an aspirin make you feel better, honey?"

"I've already looked. You're out of aspirin."

"Well, I'll go get some." Jack dressed then jumped in his corvette and made for the store a few miles away.

Through the kitchen window Theresa watched him drive off. "Why am I staying with him?" she muttered, "Why do I bother? What am I getting out of this relationship besides an occasional orgasm?"

Jack pulled up to the convenience store and turned off the engine. He sat for a moment, wondering what was different about the day. The sunlight seemed to have a new quality about it, something he just couldn't put his finger on. It seemed to be not only rich, golden and warm, as it is on especially lovely days, but it also seemed almost liquid and flowed about everything it touched in gentle currents. There was something surreal about the trees. There was a luxurious quality to the leaves that reminded him of cool, green velvet. On the way the wind had poured through his open windows like a torrent of water from a mountain stream. He had felt as if he were swimming in a river of chilled chardonnay. The store's white wall blazed like the flame from an immense arc welder. The red and green in its corporate sign were so rich it seemed as if the color were about to drip like fresh paint, although it was obvious that the sign was only colored plastic.

A dark, Persian face peered out from the store window with a look of curiosity then disappeared. A shudder swept down Jack's spine. Jack couldn't understand why he felt such heart stopping fear, and then remembered the dream. The clerk reminded Jack of the man pushing the wheelbarrow of flayed skins; it wasn't him, but the resemblance was uncanny. "Bullshit", Jack muttered.

Jack found it hard not to stare at the clerk as he entered and glanced around for the medicines section. The clerk stared back, not saying a word and not smiling. Jack suspected that the clerk was waiting to see if Jack stole anything. The suspicion irritated Jack. It made him feel dirty and for making him feel dirty, Jack hated the clerk. Jack found the medicines section and snatched up the closest bottle of aspirin. He walked up to the clerk, taking wide, forceful steps. The clerk kept his eyes on Jack. Jack wanted to punch the clerk in the mouth for making him feel dirty. He wanted an excuse to punch him in the nose and watch the blood filter through his black moustache. Jack set the bottle of aspirin on the counter.

The clerk fixed his eyes on Jack's. "Is this everything?"

"Yes." Jack returned the clerk's stare. He could feel his face tense and his jaw lock as it always did when he was angry. Jack knew he had an intense frown that signaled his anger like a flashing neon sign. The frown frightened some people, others it made tense and ready to fight, because they thought Jack was ready to fight.

"Are you sure?"

"Yes!" Jack said, raising his voice to where he thought it demanded respect and instilled a little fear as he placed his palms on the counter and leaned a few inches closer to the clerk.

The clerk backed away from Jack. "Okay! Okay! That will be three fifteen. I just wanted to know."

Jack fished in his pocket, and slapped the exact change onto the counter. He snatched the bottle from the counter and stuffed it into his jeans pocket. "Keep the receipt and the bag. I don't need any more paper in my life." Jack started toward the door.

"Asshole," muttered the clerk.

Jack whirled around and pointed a finger at the clerk's nose. "I don't need any of your fucking attitude. Do you understand?"

"Hey! This is my store! Get out or I'll call the cops, you fucking psycho!"

Jack twisted in rage. He wanted to grab the clerk by the throat and pound his head against the cash register. But then Jack noticed the security camera hidden above and behind the counter. Jack felt as if he would burst if he didn't do something, even if it was as meaningless an act as turning over the magazine and newspaper racks near the door, but he dared not do anything violent with the camera watching. Jack shot the bird at the clerk. "Go fuck yourself, asshole!"

"Asshole!" shouted the clerk. "Go to hell!"

Jack spun around and shoved the door back so hard that it swung all the way back to the limit its mechanical arm allowed. Jack threw open the car door, sat in his driver's seat, and started the engine before slamming his palms several times against the steering wheel. He threw the corvette into reverse, whipped out of the parking space, and sped down the street. Jack fumed and swore all the way home.

Entering the kitchen, Jack slammed the door behind him. On the refrigerator was a note: "Jack — I've gone shopping with Betty & Jeanette. Maybe to happy hour later. Fix your own supper. I may not be back by then. —T".

Bitch, thought Jack. This is typical. I go out of my way for her and she takes off without a word. Jesus, how inconsiderate! As soon as I find a richer broad, I'm dumping Theresa's narrow ass. Damn! Jack punched the refrigerator scattering magnets, recipes, and photos.

Jack knew he needed to relax and to forget about the clerk. He got a beer from the fridge, got his cigarettes and matches from the kitchen table, went into the living room, put an X-rated tape into the VCR, and flopped down in his easy chair. He couldn't get into the movie because visions of grabbing the clerk by the hair and slamming his face several times into the cash register kept racing through his mind over and over. Every time Jack lit a cigarette a screaming man appeared in the match flame and startled him. Jack went over to his computer and tried going through his e-mail and reviewing the accounts from the trucking company he owned, but he could not get over his rage. He rose and paced back and forth muttering repeatedly "Asshole, fucking asshole".

Jack glanced through the window and saw the mail truck pulling away. Good, the mail's here, he thought, maybe there will be something in that for me to do. Jack went out to the mailbox and pulled out several bills, a couple of greeting cards, and a magazine in a black plastic wrapper. Jack went back to his easy chair and flopped down in it once again. He tossed the bills and greeting cards to the side and opened the magazine. It was "American History Illustrated". Good, he thought, this might help. Jack enjoyed history.

Jack tore off the wrapper and on the cover was the caption: " Pickett's Charge at Gettysburg Valiant Effort or Incredible Blunder?" Beneath a painting of the Confederate lines being decimated point blank by rifle and artillery fire was an inset of a Matthew Brady photo showing three dead rebels. Sprawled in the foreground, face turned to the camera, was Jack's nameless companion in hell.

Jack threw the magazine across the room as if it had suddenly turned to red-hot steel. He leapt from his chair and kicked it behind the couch. It could stay there until hell froze over for all he cared. He began pacing back and forth across the room, repeatedly shifting between crossing his arms and putting his hands in his pockets. A chill ran throughout his body. He could not feel warm enough. He rubbed both arms from the shoulder to the wrist to warm them, but nothing helped.

He stopped at a window and looked out at the sunshine seeping through the leaves on the trees. Something about the light and the leaves fascinated him. The anger ebbed away in a few minutes and left Jack feeling at peace, relaxed, with his skin tingling, sensitive to the lightest touch. What's going on out there with the light and the leaves? He had never really thought about it before. He guessed that few people ever did. The light speeds from the sun in a mere eight minutes, and falls upon the leaves. The leaves, in a miraculous process, somehow consume the sunlight as food along with water and air and use it to grow and strengthen and build a tree as solid and noble as an oak. How can something as symbolic of size, strength, and solidity as an oak be made of the three most changeable and intransient substances known—light, water, and air?

I have never noticed so many beautiful things before. I know the world hasn't changed since last night; it's being just as shitty to me as it ever was. Jesus, what is it with me today? Am I going manic-depressive? One moment I'm on cloud nine, the next I'm pissed as hell.

Jack stood and gazed out the window. The south Texas sun made him feel as if he were a child again, being wrapped in a warm, flannel blanket by his mother. Jack leaned forward, rested his forehead against the cool glass, and closed his eyes for a moment. He drummed his fingers on the windowsill. He felt relaxed, drowsy, mildly drunk, but with an underlying current of energy, as if he had had too much caffeine. He massaged his forearms, and then rubbed his shoulders to release the last bits of tension. He massaged his neck and ran his fingers through his hair. He felt incredibly good. He stretched and twisted from side to side. He turned to the center of the room, and took a step, and then he skipped. He skipped again. He skipped across the room. He placed both palms on the floor, and then stood on his hands with his legs out straight and his heels against the wall. Pocket change went cascading out of his jeans and onto the carpet. Jack did three vertical push-ups and placed his feet on the floor and somersaulted backward into the center of the carpet. He had not done a vertical push-up or a somersault in twenty years. He felt renewed, vigorous. He had also felt a large, thick object push up into his right buttock as he had rolled across the carpet: his wallet. Jack took the wallet out of his hip pocket and laid it on a coffee table nearby.

He glanced around at the room from his new perspective on the carpet. Only the sunlight coming through the window seemed to give him real pleasure today. In comparison, the flat-screen TV, the high-powered stereo system, the high-priced DVD player, the eighty-gigabyte PC with the flat-screen monitor, offered only vague and twisted distortions of reality. Jack knew now that he would not be happy until he got outside into the fresh air under the clear, blue sky and among the rustling leaves, the cool grass, and the flowing sunshine. But that would be only a beginning. There was something more he desired, but he couldn't quite put his finger on it. There was something in the back of his mind that drove this energy that forced the blood faster through his veins. Jack sprang to his feet, and glanced around the room, but could not figure it out.

Then he saw on the mantle a framed photo of Theresa standing in the surf fishing on the day they had gone camping on Padre Island. They had found a deserted stretch of beach and pitched a tent. There was no other human within sight for the entire day. At night, their driftwood campfire, the Milky Way, and an occasional falling star provided the only light as they made love again and again. That was what he wanted.

He wanted to make love. He did not want just sex. He was not interested in his own orgasm as much as he felt an over-powering desire for the smooth texture of Theresa's skin; the velvety brush of her nipples across his face; the sight of the light playing upon the delicate, minute hair covering the back of her neck; the tickle of her breath as it flowed around the contours of his ear. Above all else, he wanted to hear her voice, that voice that sometimes changed into a shrill nag when he wasn't paying attention to what she said, or when he forgot to pick up something at the store, or when he neglected to call and tell her he would be late for supper. Now it dawned on him: over the years she had put up with a lot more crap than she should have. He wanted to apologize.

Jack reached for the phone, but saw Theresa's cell phone lying next to it. Theresa's note had said that she would be at happy hour, which meant she would be at Alexandra's. Happy hour was from four to seven, and it was almost four now. Jack grabbed his cigarettes and was out the door.

When Jack walked into Alexandra's it was crowded, but it wasn't crammed shoulder to shoulder as on Saturday nights. It was small, with maybe a maximum capacity of a hundred and fifty, with brick walls, and a U-shaped mahogany bar with brass trim and a brass foot rail. There was a jukebox and several tables and booths, but not enough room for a band or dance floor. Everything was polished, clean, and well organized. Two bartenders in white shirts with black bow ties, supported by a short bar back in a black polo shirt, handled all the customers. It was one of the coziest, nicest, and most expensive bars in town.

Jack looked over the crowd, but saw neither Theresa nor her friends. Might as well have a beer and wait a while, thought Jack, there are worse things that could happen to a guy. Jack took a seat at the bar and a tall, thin, blonde bartender with a pockmarked face came over.

"How can I help you?" The bartender was not happy; he had a stern, unsmiling expression with a somber tone.

"I'll have a pint of Bass."

The bartender took a step, poured the Bass, and set it in front of Jack. "That'll be three ten."

Jack reached into his pocket, and found that he had left his wallet at home, but he had a wad of cash. Jack gave the man a five.

"Keep the change?"

Jack couldn't believe the man had the balls to ask for over a sixty per cent tip for taking a step. "No."

The bartender got the change, set it in front of Jack, and walked off to another customer without a word; his impertinence was taking the shine off the wonderful mood Jack was experiencing. Jack sipped his ale with an electric tension gathering inside. He lit another cigarette and the little screaming man in the match flame startled him again.

When he finished his beer, Jack ordered another from the same surly bartender, who was apparently responsible for Jack's side of the bar. The bartender brought it, set it in front of Jack, and said "three ten". Jack gave him three dollar bills and a dime. The bartender took it without a word or a glance at Jack. This added a little fuel to the fire smoldering in Jack, who was growing tired of waiting for Theresa. Jack pulled out his cell phone and tried calling home, but no one answered.

Jack's pocket was weighted with a few dollars in change including that from the convenience store. Jack felt he could wait a while longer for Theresa, but not very much longer. He left his pint at the bar, went to the jukebox, and put in all the change he could plus a couple of dollar bills. While the music played, Jack finished his ale, then ordered a third and a fourth, each time going through the same surly ritual with the bartender, each time paying in exact change, each time lighting a cigarette and being startled by the little man, and each time calling home with no result.

For his fifth pint, Jack dug into his pocket and discovered that he had only three dollars left and about a dozen pennies. Jack laid the three bills on the bar and started counting out the pennies.

Suddenly the bartender whipped his arm straight out, pointed at the door, and shouted, "Get out!"

"What?"

"Get out of my bar!"

"Fuck you! I haven't done anything—

"You don't tell me to fuck myself in my bar! Get out of my fucking bar!"

"You goddamned son of a bitch—

"Get out of my bar or I'll call the fucking cops!"

"Where's the manager? I want the fucking manager!"

"Get out of my goddamned bar, you son of a bitch!"

Through a doorway on the opposite side of the bar Jack

spotted a young man in a black suit in a hallway leading to an adjacent restaurant and guessed he was the manager. Jack brushed through the crowd, and shoved his raging face to within a foot of the manager's. "I want to talk to you about your fucking bartender. That son of a bitch just threw me out for not tipping. I've been to hundreds of bars in my life and this is the only time I have been thrown out for not tipping! What kind of fucking business are you running here?"

The manager stood quietly erect and emotionless, listening to Jack's tirade with a professional and dispassionate interest. At one point he gently raised his right hand to chest level and motioned for someone behind Jack to stay put.

Jack glanced over his right shoulder and saw a huge, well-dressed, bald man of about thirty that could easily have been a pro-wrestler at his day job. He had taken a step toward Jack and, judging by the intense look contorting his face, was ready for a vicious fight, until the manager stopped him with the gentle, halfhearted wave. Jack wouldn't have cared if the bald man had charged screaming. Jack wanted a fight. He needed to release the tension that was boiling over. Jack stood quaking in fury, his right knee trembling, his large hands knotted into tight fists. As Jack flashed his face to the bouncer, he detected a moment of apprehension in the big man's eyes, a look that told Jack the big man had a touch of fear, and that told Jack that the fight would have gone to Jack. At that point Jack had no fear, only a passion to destroy anything even vaguely connected to the bartender. All other emotions and desires vanished.

Jack turned back to the manager. "What the hell are you going to do about this? You need to fire the son of a bitch."

"I'm sorry, sir. We have had complaints about the man before, and there's nothing we can do about it."

"Nothing you can do about it! Fire the son of a bitch! I can't believe he's any damn good for your business."

"I'm sorry, sir."

Jack started waving his forefinger in the manager's face. "Goddammit, give me the owner's name. I'll call him and see what he can do about it."

"I'm sorry, sir. I'm not allowed to do that."

"You motherfucker! Give me the owner's name and his number or I'll find out and take your fucking name to him too, you little shit."

"I'm sorry, sir. I'm not allowed to do that."

Jack started thumping his finger against the manager's chest. "You cocksucker! So help me God, I will make some calls tomorrow and I am going to do my damnedest to find out who owns this gyp joint and I am taking you, Brad Emerson," Jack said reading from the manager's name tag, "and that fucking piece of shit bartender up to him myself, you cocksucker! Jack whirled about and stomped out the door, vowing vengeance on the lot of them.

When Jack got home, he found a note from Theresa on the door. "Jack, I have decided I need some time away from you. Don't bother calling my mother's. I won't be there. Don't ask Betty or Jeanette either. They won't tell you where I am. I just need some time to sort things out. I have packed everything I need. You can keep the rest of my stuff. Maybe I will be back some day. —T"

Jack was now nearly paralyzed with fury. He wanted to scream, rage, throw furniture, raise havoc, and wreak destruction, but he knew all of these were futile gestures that would only hurt his own world and do nothing to alleviate the suffering he felt. He went into the living room, sat in his easy chair, and gazed into the growing darkness of a far corner as night enveloped the unlit house. For hours he sat in the same transfixed pose trembling with anger, searching his mind for a solution to bring his world back into order. There was nothing he could do about Theresa except await her return, if she decided to return. The bartender was another matter.

People like that bartender are no damn good, thought Jack. He's got his whole fucking organization protecting his sorry ass, so there's no reason he should not go on being an asshole. Someone needs to set him aright, just on general principle, if for no other reason. And he needs to be taught a lesson quick, so he knows what he's being punished for. These sons of bitches are like dogs. If you don't punish them right away, they don't know what they are being punished for. I'll make my revenge swift and violent so he'll remember it. I'll wear a ski mask so even if he gets a look at me, he won't see anything. I'll wear old clothes and use a baseball bat so that I can burn all the evidence later. I have never killed anyone before, and I won't kill now, but I'll make him wish he were dead. The beauty of this is that he will suspect it was me, because of the argument today, but there won't be any evidence, so there's nothing anyone can do. There are probably a lot of others that he has pissed off as well, so I won't be the only suspect. The manager said they had had complaints about him before. He'll never be able to know for certain who did it. He'll have to either start being a nicer guy or get out of the bartending business. Either way I win. I might even be able to rub a little salt into the wound literally as well as figuratively. He can suspect it's me, but if nothing is proven, I'll go back to his bar and drop subtle hints about it maybe happening again. If he tries a cheap shot like spitting into my beer, he'll keep paying the price until he learns who is in control.

Jack stood, went to his bar, and fixed himself an Irish whiskey on the rocks. He ambled over to the window and gazed out at the night. The sunbeam was long gone. The live oak was a silhouette. Night wrapped everything in it cool, black beauty, but it wasn't the beauty of the sunbeam. This was an otherworldly beauty of the type found in ancient forests, on the sea before dawn, or in a tomb. I like the darkness, thought Jack. I feel better with it rather than with that shit with the sunbeam earlier. What was that? What has been happening to me?

Jack nursed his whiskey for an hour and then poured another. He lit another cigarette and told the little man in the flame to fuck off. He continued pouring and nursing his drinks until an hour before closing time. By that time he had gone through two packs of cigarettes, and he was tipsy, but he didn't think he was so drunk that he lacked the self-control to do what needed to be done. He went out to his closet and got the baseball bat he had since he was a kid. He smacked it against his palm a couple of times to remind himself of its weight. He took a stance beside an imaginary home plate, and swung at an imaginary fastball, but he obliterated a real lamp on a nearby coffee table. "Lamp was no damned good anyway," he muttered. He then got two large garbage bags from the kitchen: one to contain his bloody clothes and the other to hide the bat and to put over the bartender's head. He also got a saltshaker and put it in his pocket. Jack then went into the bedroom and changed into an old pair of jeans and a faded black polo shirt from the back of the closet. He put on the oldest pair of sneakers he had, and got the dark blue ski mask from the back of the closet's top shelf. He tried it on to get the feel of it and to see if it interfered with his vision. It did not. He took it off and crammed it into a hip pocket. He put his good clothes into the garbage bag. He would do the deed, change, put the old clothes into the bag, and toss them into a dumpster on the far side of town. The police would probably search any dumpsters near the crime scene for clues. He went to his dresser and pulled out a pair of cotton work gloves and shoved those into the other hip pocket.

Once ready, Jack went back to his bar and had a final shot and a cigarette to steady his nerves. Afterwards, his nerves were still not quite as steady as he wanted so he had another shot. He then took the bottle and poured most of the remainder into a small silver hip flask that Theresa had given him for Christmas and shoved that into his left front pocket. His head was now a bit groggy, but he decided it would be clear enough by the time he reached the bar, so it shouldn't be a problem. He grabbed his wallet and cigarettes, went out into the garage, hopped into his corvette, and headed downtown.

Jack parked a block away from Alexandra's and, leaving the bag containing his change of clothes in the car and taking the bag containing the bat, kept to the shadows as he made his way to an alley across from Alexandra's entrance just before closing. Jack guessed it would take an hour to close the place, so the bartender should come out about three. Jack hung back in the alley and tried not to look suspicious. He watched up and down the street and whenever someone appeared, he would duck behind a bush or corner. He went behind a building to light his cigarettes, so that no one would notice the flame. A thousand different details kept going through his mind. Again and again he went over a mental checklist of things he brought along to make certain he had everything he needed. He wondered if there was a back exit the bartender could use, in which case Jack might wait until dawn only to have to come back tomorrow. The thought of having to go through all this again unsettled Jack and made him a bit more nervous. Jack pulled the flask from his pocket and took a swig. What if the bartender walked out with a co-worker? This thought also made him nervous and Jack took another swig. Or what if the bartender's girlfriend picked him up every night after work? Jack might have to come out here many times before he finally got the opportunity he wanted. He took another swig. Jack's head was beginning to fog and therefore he decided to lay off the whiskey until the deed was over. He looked at his watch; he still had forty minutes to wait.

Jack lived those forty minutes in a maelstrom of doubt, fear, suspicion, boredom and, especially, terror, whenever someone approached unexpectedly from around the corner or out of nearby shadows. He had a couple of more sips, but not enough to sap his strength. Whenever he thought no one was around, Jack slipped into the shadows behind the corner of a building and had a cigarette or took a couple of practice swings at the bartender's ribs and head. Horizontal, thought Jack, I'll have to swing horizontal like I'm swinging at a baseball to get full power and to keep my balance for the next swing.

Jack checked his watch. It was almost three. Jack peeped from behind the corner where he was taking his practice swings and saw the bartender walking alone from the bar and up the street to Jack's left. Jack put the bat back into the garbage bag, took a deep breath, and walked out from his hiding place to cross the street at a quick, but quiet pace to maintain a spot about fifty feet behind the bartender.

Jack followed the bartender through the darkened streets and around a couple of corners toward an open car lot with monthly rates. The few streetlights in the area were around a bank on the other side of the lot. Jack scanned all directions and saw no one. There were no lights in any of the buildings. Jack took a deep breath, put on the mask, pulled the bat from the bag, and charged forward without a sound, bat held over his right shoulder.

The bartender heard running footsteps behind him and turned to see the bat coming for his left cheek. As the bartender fell, Jack kept pounding his head, ribs, and groin. Within a few seconds the bartender was motionless in the gutter, but Jack continued to beat the bartender's face into an unrecognizable mass for several minutes. When Jack was finally exhausted, he checked the streets again and saw no one. He lifted the mask from his head and felt the refreshing night air against his sweating face. He looked at the bartender's wide-open eyes staring motionless into different parts of the night sky.

"Well, fuck, I killed him. Hmm," muttered Jack, "I didn't use the bag, either," he added as an afterthought. Jack kicked the bag from where it lay on the sidewalk onto the corpse. He thought for a second, and then pulled out the saltshaker, uncapped it, and poured the salt on bartender's face and ground it in with his shoe.

Jack reached into his pocket and took the final draught from the flask. There was no more. Jack needed something to calm his nerves. He checked his pack and found he was out of cigarettes. He could get them at a 24-hour convenience store, but he had no cash. He looked at the bank. There was an ATM across the lot. Jack decided to quickly get the cash for the cigarettes and then high tail it back to the car to change and get the hell out. Jack put the bat back into the bag and walked over to the ATM. As he got closer to the ATM the light showed a lot of blood on his jeans and shirt. Jack kept watching in all directions, but no one approached. The streets were completely deserted. At the ATM Jack pulled out his check card, inserted it into the machine, and punched in his pin. It was then he noticed the wide-angle camera lens staring at him and which had a clear view of the lot, the murder scene, and Jack's walk from it.

"Fuck," said Jack.

Suddenly the world went black around him and Jack awoke naked, writhing in pain in a puddle of sewage and vomit at the edge of a fiery lake in the depths of hell as thousands of miserable souls milled around him. The raw-boned man stood muttering to the side and staring at Jack.

"It's the game. The game. Y'know, the game. If they beat you constantly, you'll get used to it. But if they let you rest, oh, this is vicious, yes it is, let you rest once in a while to catch your breath, send you back to the world to enjoy being alive, it makes it harder to start again. They even make you notice things you never noticed before and enjoy the world as you never enjoyed it before, just so that it will be that much harder for you to return. Agony. Agony. Pure agony. And and and all the time you're resting, they're reminding you in little ways that you got to come back." His voice trailed off, almost weeping. He stopped clawing and scratching and stared at the burning sea, muttering, "They're masters. Yes, masters, masters. You never get used to the torment. Never do. The suffering is always fresh."

Just as Jack stood up, gazing in disbelief at the man and the surroundings, he heard a voice shout "You!" from the morass of the damned to his left. He turned in time to see the bartender run toward him and leap, tackling Jack about the waist. Both rolled, kicking and clawing and punching, down an embankment into the fiery surf.

3

Dream Warrior

Laid out on the crude wooden table in front of Miguel were corn tortillas, roasted rabbit, a large bowl of pinto beans, and something unrecognizable made of dried corn. The old man sitting across the table from him seemed as anachronistic as the meal: long, thick, silver hair; narrow slits for eyes; leathery skin that seemed more fit on a shrunken head; a dirty headband; and a serape. Through the light of the kerosene lanterns and the logs burning in the fireplace, Miguel looked around at the objects hanging from the walls of the cabin: skulls of cattle, rattlesnake skins, coyote hides, a Bowie knife, bunches of dried chiles, ceremonial rattles, and paintings of human sacrifice that looked like they had been copied from Aztec temples. The flickering firelight made the figures seem alive, as if the priests were slicing and stabbing their prisoners over and over.

Miguel struggled for something to say. He had seen the old man only a few times in his life and the last of those was twelve years ago, when Miguel was eight. "So, great-grandfather, Dad tells me you're a sorcerer?"

"Some call me a sorcerer." The man's voice was cracked and hoarse. "I am a Nahuatl priest."

"Nahuatl?"

"They are called Aztec these days, but the Aztecs were only one of several Nahuatl peoples. Pass me the goddamned corn, please."

"Oh, sure." Miguel picked up the bowl of dried corn and handed to the old man.

"And don't call me great-grandfather. That makes me sound too old. Just call me grandfather...or *sir*. I like *sir*." The old man scooped out some corn onto his plate with a wooden spoon. Then he licked the spoon, left it in the bowl of corn, and passed it back to Miguel. Miguel set it to the side while the old man spoke with his mouth full. "You don't speak Spanish?"

"A little. We don't need it that much in Corpus Christi."

"Englishthe language of goddamned interlopers. They will be gone one day and the land will revert to the natives."

Miguel did not understand, but felt it polite to agree. "Uh, yeah. Okay."

"So you got in trouble in Texas and like any other *gringo* you came to Mexico. What did you do? Kill someone?"

"Well, no. I tried to kill someone, but

"What's the matter? Couldn't you shoot straight? You should have used a knife." The old man picked up a butcher knife lying on the table and jabbed it toward Miguel as if he were sticking it into an unseen enemy's ribs and twisting it. "It takes more guts to use a knife and get his blood on you.

You actually have to get close and touch the son of a bitch. It makes you a warrior. Where did you screw up?"

"I, uh, missed, and hit a tree next to him."

"That's the bad thing about guns. You can miss with a gun. You can't miss with a knife though. Unless you're a complete idiot, you'll hit something. No, I can't say that. Unless you're an idiot, you'll hit something. A complete idiot will fall on his own knife. What did this *pendejo* do to you?"

"Well, it's hard to talk about." Miguel paused, holding back some tears and keeping his voice from cracking. "My fiancée, Cristina, knew this guy, Sonny, from high school. I knew him too—at one time—but that's not important now. She goes—went to Texas A&M, and he's a real sleaze bag, but she went to buy some grass off him for her and a couple of her girlfriends. She knew he was a piece of shit, but she never expected him to harm her. Well, anyway, when she was at his apartment, he offered her some iced tea he had laced with some kind of date rape drug. Then he called his friends, Paco and Stevie, out of the back room and they gangbanged her and beat her up. She was in the hospital for a long time, a lot of it in the psycho ward. She wouldn't let anyone touch her. She would just start screaming. She wouldn't talk to the cops, because the shitheads told her after they had finished with her, that they would rape her and her friends until they all died, if the cops ever came around asking questions. After the hospital released her, she told me all about it, and then, a few days later, she killed herself with sleeping pills." Miguel fought hard to hold back the tears.

"Then next night I hid in some bushes outside a strip

joint and when Sonny and his buddies came out, I emptied a Beretta at them. They weren't far off, but I was so nervous I didn't hit a damn thing. They recognized me and shouted my name. They chased me for a while, but I got away. Dad said I should come down here and stay with you until things cooled down some and I could get a grip on myself."

"*Qué pinches cabrones,*" muttered the old man. "You are doing the right thing by not weeping like a little girl. Don't ever cry. Be a man. Be macho. Get revenge. Make those *pendejos* weep."

While Miguel was regaining his composure, he looked at the distant wall behind the old man and saw a photo of Geronimo kneeling and holding a rifle. "Mom says you actually knew Geronimo."

"Naw, I didn't know him. Met him once. At the Saint Louis World's fair. He autographed that picture on the wall behind me. He killed my uncle before that. Killed him slow. Tied him to a wagon wheel, poured tar on him, and lit it. Geronimo hated Mexicans more than he hated the gringos."

"How old are you, grandfather?"

"My mother told me I was born in eighteen eighty-four. She lied a lot though. Wait here."

The old man rose slowly and unsteadily from his chair. Miguel stood and reached across the table to steady him.

"Get your hands off me," the old man snapped. "I can still get around. Hell, I still go to the cathouse in Chihuahua at least once a month. Ask the whores."

"What keeps you going, grandfather?"

The old man smiled and turned to look out the window

at the moon rising in the night above the silhouetted pines lining the ridges. "There are some plants even better than peyote, if you know how to use them. Maybe I will teach you." The old man's smile slowly vanished and he let his head droop toward his chest. He lifted it again with a somber expression. "But first, I must teach you how to kill and not be caught. If I can give nothing else to my only great-grandson in this life, I will give this. With this way, you cannot miss."

The old man walked over to the refrigerator and pulled out a couple of limes and then went to the cupboard near the stove, opened it, and pulled out two shot glasses and a clear gallon jug containing some dark twisting object, like a large coil, immersed in an amber fluid. He came back and set the limes and shot glasses next to the saltshaker on the table. When the old man set the jug down, Miguel saw that the coil was a rattlesnake almost two feet long and preserved in tequila. "But tonight," said the old man smiling for the first time that night, "I shall teach you how to drink." As the old man poured two shots, he looked into Miguel's eyes and saw fear mixed with bewilderment. "You are afraid."

"No, sir."

"You're lying more to yourself than to me. This time, I do not mind your lying to me. A man should never let anyone know that he is afraid, but you should never lie to yourself. If you lie to me again, depending on the lie, I may beat you or throw you out of my house. Agreed?"

Miguel was too frightened to say anything but a respectful "Yes, sir."

"Good. Understand there is nothing wrong with being afraid. Fear is the gods' way of telling us not to do something stupid that will get us killed. But you must master your fear. And before you can master someone else you must master yourself. That is what killing is: mastering someone else. Understand?"

Miguel felt he should agree, but also felt that would be a lie. "No, sir."

"Good. You did not lie." The old man sliced up a lime and pushed a few pieces over to Miguel with his knife blade. Together, each rubbed a slice on the back of his hand below the thumb and sprinkled salt on it as the old man continued to talk. "I shall teach you to be a dream warrior and to kill with sorcery. Are you afraid?"

"Yes, sir."

"Good. You should be. Sorcery can kill you as easily as it can kill others. Sorcery demands complete mastery of yourself, because you must master not only your thoughts, but also your dreams." The old man raised his shot glass in a toast. "*Salud.*"

Miguel returned the toast. "Salud."

Each licked some salt from his hand, downed the tequila, and bit a slice of lime. The old man poured another round. "You drink well," he said. "If you cannot master alcohol, if you cannot drink and not get drunk, you cannot master yourself." They did another round and the old man poured two more shots. "The final test will be hell. For that you must have mastery over your actions, your thoughts, your dreams, your emotions, and your desires. At point, you must ask yourself how badly you want to be a sorcerer. To pass the test, you will have to make a great sacrifice that will change you forever. Are you afraid?"

"Yes, sir."

"Good. Very good."

"What is the final test?"

"You will find out if the time comes."

Two years later Miguel was sitting at home with his parents over a dinner of tamales, charro beans, and guacamole. It was his first night back.

"You're lucky to have gotten to know your great-grandfather," said Miguel's dad. "Not many people get that chance."

"It seems that everyone I love in this life dies."

"Everyone dies. That's part of life," said Miguel's mom. "Everything changes. Why, look at yourself. You've changed. You're tan and lean and healthy and there's something else—"

"He's quiet," said Miguel's father looking at him and thinking hard. "He's more contemplative. He thinks more—a lot more than he used to. He thinks things throughnot impulsive like he used to be. He's more confident too. Those are signs of maturity."

"Great-grandfather taught me a lot. More than anyone will ever know. The mountains taught me a lot too. Life is very different without TV or radio or electricity. You learn what is important." Miguel paused. "I think I'll go for a walk."

"Will you be gone long?"

"Probably. I'm still thinking a lot about great-grandfather." This was true, but Miguel knew the task he had to accomplish would take a few hours, and if he told his parents that, they would ask questions he did not want to answer.

"We'll probably be in bed by the time you get back. Good night, Miguel."

"Good night, Mom. Good night, Dad."

"Good night, son," said his dad.

As Miguel started out of the kitchen, he looked through the glass in the door of one cupboard and saw his dad's Mezcal with a gusano worm in the bottle. "I don't understand why anyone would drink anything with a worm in the bottle," he said to his parents. "The only good stuff contains a rattlesnake."

Miguel went up to his room, picked up a red backpack, and headed out of the house. The night was warm and clear and Miguel could see many of the brightest stars, though the city lights blocked out most. He walked a couple of blocks to the end of the street, where he started upon a short path that led into a park. At the juncture of the path with a broad, paved trail, Miguel looked around. The park was empty and lit only by a single streetlight a short distance away to the left on the edge of a small, empty parking lot. Miguel followed the trail a few feet to the right, where it turned sharply left and led over a low rise into a small wood of mesquite, palmetto, and a few short ash. To his right, a sign stated: "Park curfew 10:00 p.m." and several yards beyond that lay the broad expanse of Oso Bay lit only by the lights of Texas A&M University on the opposite shore about a mile away, and by the lights of the naval air station beyond that. A hundred yards into the woods, Miguel came to a short square post labeled "ASH"
to the right of the trail under a short ash tree on the edge of a large open area bordering the bay. Miguel opened his

backpack, took out a small flashlight, and turning right into the weeds and tall grass walked several yards off the trail. He had chosen this spot earlier in the day, because it was a good distance from the paths, where the pairs of lovers of all sexual orientations normally strolled or made out. Also, it almost always had a breeze, which he felt to be important not only to his state of mind for the ritual, but because one of the Nahuatl gods he would be praying to was Tezcatlipoca, the god of the night and of the wind. Miguel turned off the flashlight, took a seat among the glasswort in the edge of the mudflat bordering the bay, and opened his backpack. He felt around inside it. He felt the obsidian mirror and then found the maguey thorn he would need. He also took out a bag of ololiuqui seeds, a gourd of pulque liquor, some resin known as copal, a few sheets of paper, and a cigarette lighter. He rose to his knees, took a deep breath, and began chanting a long prayer in Nahuatl.

Miguel finished the ritual about four hours later. He looked at the cuts he had inflicted on his forearms with the maguey thorns and wondered how he would explain them to his mother. Long sleeves could cover them for the next few days while he searched for an apartment. After he got a job and moved out, the wounds would cease to be a problem. He wouldn't need to do the ritual much longer anyway—just until Sonny and his friends were dead.

Miguel rose and started to walk back to his home. The interesting part of the murder would begin after he went to bed, he thought, but he was so excited about it, yet nervous at the same time, he didn't know how long it would be before he could fall asleep. He would have to use the tricks for falling asleep his great-grandfather had taught him. He wouldn't be able to use sleeping pills. "No gringo medicines," his grandfather had said, "only the roots and herbs I have shown to you; anything else will only interfere."

Miguel missed his great-grandfather. It had taken a long time to get used to his personal habits and even longer to understand where he was coming from, but with time he had come not only to respect the old man, but to love him as well. Ironically, Miguel had had to overcome that love in order to pass his final test and earn the respect of the old man.

When Miguel arrived home the lights were out. He decided to enter through the kitchen so as not to awaken his parents. He opened the back door and started across the linoleum floor, when a shadowy figure sitting at the kitchen table moved and startled him.

"Relax," said the shadow. "Have a seat and talk for a minute." It was Miguel's father. He switched on the lamp above the table. Miguel's father was in his undershirt and pajama bottoms. He had three empty cans of Tecate in front of him along with a saltshaker and slices of lime.

As Miguel took a seat his father reached into the refrigerator behind him and pulled out two more cans. He pushed one over to Miguel and together they added salt and lime and took a drink. "Son," said his father, "I am guessing your great-grandfather Guadalupe taught you some of his magic."

"He taught me all of it."

Miguel's dad let out a deep breath as he thought for a moment. "Grandfather taught it to my dad, but something in it terrified him and he quit before he learned everything, and he never taught it to me. He talked about it very little. All I know about it is that anyone who knows it can kill with impunity. That is a tremendous responsibility, because, if you want to, you can kill on a whim and no one other than another Nahuatl sorcerer can do anything about it. To be honest, I am afraid the temptation might be too much for you, son. I don't want to see you turn into an evil man—a monster."

"Don't worry. I won't, dad. Grandfather hammered self-control into me constantly and a big part of the reason he did so was to prevent that. In his way, I think he loved me and he tried to teach me everything he could to help me live a good, long, happy life."

"Do you have any qualms about killing?"

"Sometimes. It's not because of the hurt I'll inflict on them though. It's because of the suffering their parents and relatives will go through because of their deaths. They're not guilty of any crime, but they're going to hurt."

"Yeah. I remember how grandfather suffered when dad was killed."

"Killed? You never told me he was killed."

"He was killed by a man named Benny in an argument over a poker game. The police caught Benny that night and locked him up. I suspect your great-grandfather killed him, because the next night Benny was sleeping in his cell when he suddenly screamed and died. The coroner never could find a reason why he died." Miguel's dad took a long drink of beer. He let out a sigh as he set the can down. "I never thought I would see the day when it would come to this between you and Sonny. You two have known each other since second grade. You used to play cops and robbers with him in our back yard. What happened? Where did you two part ways?"

"I don't know, dad. I guess we just grew apart. Sonny just kept getting more and more involved with the wrong people."

"I was always glad you didn't. You were starting to become wild yourself. Your mother and I used to lay awake at nights wondering if we were going to get a call from the police or the hospital. But then you changed. We were never so happy as when you stopped hanging out with Sonny and his crowd."

"Cristina changed me. After I met her, I never wanted to do anything that would separate us. You know what I mean?"

"Yeah. I do. I feel the same way about your mom. If what happened to Cristina happened to her, I don't know what I would do. I can't pay a visit to my grandfather." Miguel's dad took a long swig of beer. "Didn't Sonny know Cristina was your girlfriend?"

"Yeah. Maybe that's why he did it. Maybe he has something against me."

"Like what?"

"I have no idea. He's become really twisted in the last few years since he's been dealing drugs. It must be the drugs he has been using. They can screw someone up fast."

"You knew the other guys involved too, didn't you?"

"Yeah, they were a couple of years behind me and Sonny in high school. But I didn't really get to know them until a few years ago. We used to visit them at their homes, got to know their families. All that stuff."

Miguel's father nodded and said, "Well, I guess I'll go to

bed. Good night." He downed the last of his beer, rose, and went upstairs.

Miguel sat thinking about what his dad had said. When he finished his beer, he went upstairs to bed. Once Miguel was in bed, it took about half an hour of using his grandfather's techniques of emptying his mind and relaxing his body until he fell asleep. Tonight he would go after Stevie as his spirit animal, a jaguar. He was not certain what Stevie's spirit animal would be, but guessed it would be like Stevie: lean and muscular, opportunistic, clever, a scavenger of sorts, with sandy, shaggy, short hair.

In Miguel's dream, he was a jaguar running through the grasslands on Padre Island. Suddenly he emerged onto the two-lane highway and stopped. The terrain was flat, broken only by the cattails surrounding a marsh or an occasional grass-covered dune. There was no traffic on the highway. In the distance to the left the jaguar saw a coyote bolting down the remains of a deer that had been killed by a car. The coyote was facing away and upwind. He could neither see nor smell the jaguar.

The jaguar sprinted forward silently on his padded feet all the while thinking that he wanted the coyote to die slowly. When the jaguar was less than a yard from him, the coyote turned his head and saw him, but it was too late. The jaguar hit him at full speed catching the coyote's right rear leg in his jaws and crushing it. The coyote yelped as the pair tumbled together past the deer. The coyote tried to bite, but the jaguar was faster and batted his muzzle away, his claws raking down the side of the coyote's face, tearing out an eye and leaving huge gashes from his ears to the tip of his nose. The jaguar jumped back from the coyote and watched. The coyote ran as best he could on three legs down the highway, yelping and whimpering. When the coyote was about a hundred feet away, the jaguar rose and sprinted. Again, the coyote turned his face just in time to see the jaguar clamp his jaws around the remaining rear leg and crush it as the pair once again tumbled down the asphalt. Again the jaguar jumped back and sat and watched as the coyote dragged himself away whimpering and yelping. In a few minutes, the jaguar charged again and crushed the right front leg. The coyote lay on the asphalt and tried to drag himself with the remaining leg, but could not stand. The jaguar walked over and stared into the terrified coyote's eyes. The jaguar then slowly lowered his jaws and crushed the fourth leg. The jaguar looked up into the sky. The sun was directly overhead.

"Now," he said to the coyote, "I shall let you lay there and, when the sun touches the western horizon, I shall kill you. Now you understand what it is to be helpless and at the mercy of an attacker. Now you understand rape."

The coyote lay whimpering as the sun slowly dropped, turning ever-deeper shades of red. Just as it touched the horizon, the jaguar slowly lowered his head, took the coyote's yelping head into his mouth and slowly crushed it, savoring the blood spurting onto his tongue.

At that moment, Stevie awoke screaming in his bed, frightening his girlfriend, Anita, who was sleeping by his side. She tried to hold his arm and tell him it was only a nightmare, but he screamed again, thinking her hand was the jaguar's mouth closing on one of his limbs. He backhanded her, knocking her off the bed and onto the floor as he jumped out of bed to cower in a corner of the room.

Anita stood shaken and holding her now black right eye and screamed at Stevie, "You son of a bitch! I was only trying to help you!"

Stevie trembled uncontrollably.

"Jesus, man, what's wrong with you?" she asked, her contempt now turning into concern.

"I—I was a coyote and some big cat—like those you see in a zoo—it broke my legs one at a time and then bit my head."

"You mean like a lion? A tiger?"

"No, no. One with spots!"

"Like a leopard?"

"Yeah! Yeah. Like a leopard! One of those you see in the books—with the Aztecs."

"A jaguar?"

"Yeah! A jaguar!"

"Calm down, honey. It was only a dream and dreams can't hurt you, can they?"

A few days later, Miguel was standing in line at the movies when someone behind him tapped him on the shoulder. He turned and saw it was Tim, an old friend from high school that he had not seen in years. As they caught up with each other's lives (Miguel glossing over the years he spent with his great-grandfather) and news about their old classmates, Tim asked, "Say, man, did you hear about Stevie? It's all over the news tonight."

"No, I haven't seen the news. I've been getting things for my new apartment."

"They found him dead out on the island. The news is only

saying his death was gang related, but I got a cousin who was the first cop on the scene, and he said all Stevie's arms and legs had been broken and his skull was crushed, like with a vise. They found him along the road and figure he had been laying there since yesterday about sunset."

"Did they catch who did it?"

"Yeah, some guys he had done time with. They found one of their driver's licenses at the scene. When they arrested him, he gave them all up. It was all about some drug shit."

"Were Sonny and that other guy they used to hang with—

"Paco. No, they weren't involved."

"What a shame. I thought the three of them would end up in the same grave or cell or something. Oh, well. All I can say is that it couldn't have happened to a nicer guy." As Miguel sat watching the movie, he felt a wave of satisfaction and he smiled as he thought about how beautifully the spell had worked. All Miguel had to do was to kill Stevie in the dream, and the gods would kill him in a similar fashion in the real world. Just what is the real world, thought Miguel. If I kill a man in his dreams, and he dies in this world, isn't that just as real as if I killed him in this world and his dreams die? Miguel took a bite of his popcorn and thought, next time I'll try something different.

A few nights later Paco lay sleeping in his bed with his girlfriend Trish, when, in his dreams, Paco saw them lying together in bed just as they had fallen asleep. Paco believed he was awake and could not understand why he could not get to sleep. He lay there for several minutes trying to fall asleep, but could not. Then Trish rolled over to lay her head on Paco's shoulder. Paco brushed her blonde hair back from her face and saw the black eye he had given her the day before, when she had come home from the supermarket with the cheap beer he hated instead of the expensive beer he loved. Trish opened her eyes and stared at him with a smile.

"What? What?" he asked. "Why are you looking at me like that?"

Trish crawled forward until her face hung directly over his and then gently and slowly bent down until their lips touched and pressed together. She then ran the tip of her tongue down the side of his cheek and flicked it up and down his neck while her hand felt for his crotch.

"Oh! Oh! I know what you want! Yes!" Paco grinned, placed his palm against the back of her head, and pressed her face toward his groin.

Trish slipped her head from under his palm, gripped his shoulders, and rolled onto her back, pulling him on top of her.

"Oh, okay. Tonight we do it this way. But in the morning we do it the way I want." Paco lay on top of her, his weight pressing her small frame into the mattress, and wrapped his arms around her, pulling her tighter and tighter to his chest as he pressed his face against hers and, closing his eyes, forced his tongue into her mouth. As they kissed, Paco noticed Trish's tongue became huge and her teeth became long and pointed. He opened his eyes to find he was kissing a jaguar.

The jaguar growled and hissed and raked his claws down Paco's back and across his cheeks. Paco yelled and tried to push himself away, but the jaguar gripped tightly and refused to let him go. Paco reached up and gripped the jaguar's throat with both hands trying to strangle it as he tried to pound its head into the mattress. The jaguar clawed furiously. Paco pushed back hard, but the claws were too much to endure. He released the jaguar's throat, rolled across the bed, and fell onto the floor, bumping his head against his nightstand as he fell. He jerked open the nightstand's top drawer and grabbed his Glock. He stood, but as he pulled the trigger to fire the first round, the jaguar disappeared. Paco, in a panic, continued firing until he had emptied the magazine. He awoke and found he was standing beside the bed, his Glock in hand, the smell of gunpowder in the air, and Trish's bloody corpse lying on her side of the bed.

The next night Miguel and Tim met at the Club Culebra for a couple of beers. As they sat at the bar, Tim asked Miguel, "Hey, did you hear about Paco?"

"Yeah. I saw something about him on the news. He murdered his girlfriend, didn't he? Did your cousin manage to be first on the scene again?"

"No, but he was in, like, the second or third car there. A neighbor reported shooting at Paco's place and the police had half a dozen squad cars there in no time. They found Paco sitting on his porch swing in nothing but his shorts and just staring off into space still holding the pistol. My cousin said he was muttering something about a big cat and that his back and face looked like they had been clawed to pieces. Anyway, they could see the gun was empty because the slide was back and so they took it from him and hauled him off. Inside his house, they found he had emptied the magazine into his girlfriend. They figure he tried to rape her and she put up a fight, because they found his skin under her fingernails. There was blood everywhere."

"Well," said Miguel, "all I can say is that they deserved each other. Neither was worth a damn and, from what I hear, they were running a crystal meth lab out of that house."

"That's what the cops found. The garage was one big meth lab. With Paco dead and Stevie dead, I wonder how long it will be before Sonny is dead."

"Probably not long."

Miguel and Tim drank for a while at the Culebra until closing time and then parted, Tim walking south along Chaparral Street and Miguel walking north. As Miguel approached Darla's Bar along a dark section of street, he saw a large, muscular man with a thick neck and stooped shoulders lumber out, staggering a little with his head down, and coming toward Miguel. Miguel kept walking ahead thinking that, considering how much he had changed and with his face toward the ground, Sonny would not recognize him, if he could recognize anyone, considering how drunk he appeared. Miguel found he could not keep himself from staring at Sonny as he drew closer. He felt a combination of morbid curiosity, intense hatred, and unspeakable contempt kept his eyes focused on Sonny. He wanted to look away, but could not.

When Miguel's feet appeared within Sonny's field of vision, Sonny snapped his head up at Miguel and shouted, "What the fuck are you looking at?" Miguel remained silent and continued to walk on, but could not tear his eyes from Sonny. Sonny suddenly lunged at Miguel, gripped his throat with both hands, and pinned him against the wall of a parking garage in the darkness where a small tree blocked off the sickly glow from the nearest streetlight. Miguel grasped Sonny's wrists and tried to break his grip, but Sonny was too strong and his thick forearms felt like wire cables. Sonny moved his face so close to Miguel's, that Miguel could see the capillaries in Sonny's eyes and he could smell the beer and jalapeños on his breath and the sweat on his face and hands. "I asked you, what th'fuck are you looking at?"

Sonny's meaty hands were beginning to crush Miguel's throat and Miguel's breathing was becoming more labored and raspy and shallow. Miguel tried to answer, but his words came out only as a series of gurgles. Miguel slipped his right hand into his front pocket. He found his ballpoint pen and pushed its cap off with his thumb. He pulled it out and held it in his fist with its point toward Sonny's heart. Miguel moved the pen forward as far as he could in his fist so that he could plunge it as deeply as possible into Sonny's solar plexus. If he angled the pen just right, he figured he might be able to stick it at least partially into Sonny's heart.

A puzzled look came across Sonny's face, and he asked, "Hey, don't I know you?" Just then someone down the street broke out into loud laughter and Sonny jerked his face toward the sound. Miguel glanced as far as he could toward the laughter as well and just beyond the laughing man he saw a police car slowly cruising in their direction. Its lights were not flashing and so the officers inside had not yet seen Sonny choking Miguel. Either Sonny had seen it clearly enough or something else entered his drunken mind so he decided to let go of Miguel. He put his hands into his pocket, and walked away from the approaching cruiser with his head down.

Miguel leaned against the wall and tried to catch his breath. He knew Sonny's grip would leave bruises around his neck. He rubbed the areas Sonny's hands had gripped, and tried to work out the remaining pain and stiffness. "Yeah, you know me, you son of a bitch. I was best man at your wedding. It will be interesting to meet your spirit animal."

As he was able to breathe again, Miguel knew he would have to be more careful in his dream battles. That was the danger in dreams, his grandfather had taught him, not only could you kill them in their dreams, they could also kill you. Now he had experienced that for the first time. Paco had gripped Miguel's throat in last night's dream and now Sonny had gripped it in this world.

A few nights later, while entering Sonny's dream, Miguel felt as if he were entering a kaleidoscope made of fragments of neon, black lights, strobe lights, raging fires, and shards of warped and blurred memories of childhood abuse, fistfights, blood, hatred, fear, terror, shock, and a hundred petty crimes. Sonny's mind was a constantly spinning jumble of night-mares. Miguel assumed his jaguar form and cautiously stayed in the background of each scene, searching for Sonny's spirit animal. As of yet, he had not seen Sonny in the dream. He had seen only Sonny's subconscious. The scenes were so frag-mented and changed so rapidly that even though Miguel rec-ognized himself in many, he did not have the time to pinpoint the events. Then the nightmares gradually became fewer and did not change as rapidly. The roulette wheel of Sonny's mind was slowing. Miguel began to recognize bits and pieces.

Miguel saw the day they first met in second grade. He saw the nights during grade school when he stayed over at Sonny's home and Sonny would sneak cigarettes after his par-ents had gone to bed. He glimpsed the day Sonny and he tried out for high school football. He relived the evening Sonny cried on Miguel's shoulder when his first girlfriend broke his heart and when Sonny called him to say he had been arrested for stealing a car. He saw himself and Sonny rolling bums for change and selling dope. There was Sonny dating Julie and then there was Sonny cheating on Julie and hiding Polaroids in his garage. He saw the first time they sold a kilo of pot and then a kilo of cocaine. Miguel relived Sonny's wedding with Julie, when there were only a justice of the peace and two witnesses: Miguel and Julie's sister. Sonny continued to cheat on Julie and to hide photos in his garage. Then came a series of increasingly vicious crimes, fear of being caught, anger once caught, more fear in front of the judge, terror and more anger in jail, and frustration at no one hiring him once out. Julie became involved in the drug dealing and fencing stolen property and all the time Sonny cheated on her and hid more photos. He also hid money from her as well as love letters to other women in a toolbox in the toolshed. Miguel saw the day he had told Sonny he was going straight to keep Cristina. He saw Sonny becoming increasingly violent and beating or knifing people who cheated him. His crimes grew in intensity and viciousness until, finally, the rape.

Miguel hid his eyes and tried to shut out the sounds of the rape, but it did no good. He wept on the outside while raging inside. He sickened and felt his own hatred and anger would rip him apart. Then the rape was over. It was night and Stevie and Paco were carrying Cristina out to Stevie's car while Sonny stood in his doorway and said, "Dump her on Leopard Street with the other whores. I'll teach Miguel to tell me to fuck off. I'll be doing the fucking and I'll fuck anyone I want."

That was the reason. The week before the rape Sonny had asked Miguel to come along as added back up when he was going to buy a kilo of cocaine from a guy downtown. He wanted Miguel to take a rifle and to hide in some bushes near the meeting spot. Miguel told him no, that he had given up that life because he didn't want to do anything that would cause Cristina to leave him. Sonny insisted again and again and Miguel had refused each time until he became fed up and had told Sonny to fuck off. Sonny only stared at Miguel in reply, turned his back, and walked off. Miguel knew that was when to fear Sonny most. When he was about to avenge himself, he never threatened anyone, so that no one could ever testify that he had made a threat and so that no one could prepare for what was about to happen. Sonny simply let his actions speak for him and that would be the threat for the next poor bastard. But Miguel never expected Sonny to take out his anger on someone uninvolved. He thought he had known Sonny, but he was wrong. Sonny had become more evil than Miguel had ever suspected.

Each scene became progressively darker as Sonny aged. Soon Miguel found himself in complete darkness. But with his jaguar eyes, darkness did not prevent Miguel from seeing what was there to see. Then he heard crackling and popping from the ground to his left. He looked over and saw that a large section of the surface on which he was walking had dropped away and formed a high cliff. At the base of the cliff flames sprung up from what appeared to be a lava bed. Sonny's dreams had shifted from fragmented memories to the current state of his soul.

Miguel heard something shuffling across the ground behind him. He turned and saw a pair of eyes sparkling with the reflections of the firelight coming from the pit. They stood a few feet off the ground at the top of a hazy, monstrous silhouette. Whatever Sonny's spirit animal was, it was big and stood on its hind legs. The creature shuffled forward quickly and his eyes moved up and down, back and forth, right and left. Miguel recognized the outline of a charging gorilla and crouched, hissing and snarling.

The gorilla swung at Miguel with his open palm, but Miguel was faster and ducked under the blow and sprang behind Sonny. Sonny spun with his open hand extended, trying to backhand Miguel, but Miguel ducked again and once more sprang behind Sonny. This time however, he saw his opportunity and leapt upon Sonny's shoulders, digging his in claws to hold on as Sonny flailed and twisted trying to grab him. Miguel then opened his jaws and clamped his teeth into Sonny's skull, trying to crush it as jaguars normally kill their prey, but Sonny's skull was too big and Miguel could not fit it into his mouth as he wanted. He chomped down and Sonny howled, but did not die; he only flailed and spun more furiously. Suddenly, Miguel felt Sonny's thick paw grasp his tail and yank. Miguel let go of the shoulders to prevent his tail from being torn out and was flung toward the edge of the pit. Miguel hit the cliff's edge, but twisted around and grasped onto the upper surface with his front claws just as his body fell over the edge and pulled himself up and over just as Sonny charged again. Miguel tried to spring behind Sonny once again, but Sonny anticipated the move and backhanded Miguel in the ribs and sent him flying out of control into the darkness. Miguel lay on his side with several broken ribs, snarling at Sonny. Then he rose and dodged to the left as Sonny charged again trying to grasp him in a bear hug. Miguel crouched as Sonny turned again. But as Sonny charged once more, Miguel realized he would not win this fight and vanished.

Miguel entered the dreams of Julie. In her nightmare, she woke in her brass bed and could feel Sonny's weight in the bed beside her. When she turned onto her side to put her back against Sonny's, a jaguar sat by the side of her bed staring at her.

"Follow me, Julie," said the jaguar. "It is alright. I will not harm you."

Miguel led her first to the high shelf in the garage, where Sonny kept his shoebox of Polaroids of sex with hookers and with some of Julie's friends. He then took her to the toolbox in the toolshed, where Sonny stashed thousands in cash from drug deals he had not told her about and also where he stashed jewelry intended as gifts for girlfriends, inscribed with their names. Inside the box, was also a love letter to a woman named Natalie, in which he promised undying love and to get a divorce, as soon as "the stupid bitch cheats and gives me a good court case". Inside was also a silver necklace with the name "CRISTINA", which Sonny had taken as a souvenir. Julie had heard rumors Sonny had been involved in the rape, but had not believed it until now.

The jaguar then led Julie back into the garage and sat between a long rope and a five-gallon can of gasoline. The jaguar spoke. "Look at the scars he has given you, Julie. Every time you glance at another man you take a beating. He is not worthy of the love and sacrifice you have given him. But if you leave him, he gets what he wants and he is free to terrorize more women. Do what you have to. Have the strength. Do not fear. Put aside all thoughts of anything or anyone else and do what you have to do."

Julie awoke from her dream sweating. She looked at Sonny laying spread eagle on the bed, one arm over her head and one leg across hers. She carefully lifted Sonny's leg, swung her feet onto the floor, and placed the leg gently upon the mattress. She crept into the garage and found the shoebox of Polaroids. She went to the toolshed and found the toolbox with the cash, jewelry, necklace, and letter. She then went back to the garage and found the rope and gasoline.

In a few minutes, Sonny tried to roll over in his sleep, but found he could not move. He awoke and discovered he was tied hand and foot with rope to the brass bed. Julie stood above him holding a can of gasoline. Before he could ask what she was doing, Julie began pouring the gasoline upon Sonny's face and chest. He squeezed his eyes shut tightly, but gasoline had already gotten in and he screamed. Gasoline flowed into his mouth and he choked. The minute it took Julie to pour the gasoline seemed to last forever, but it was not long enough, when Sonny felt the bed go up in flames.

When Miguel awoke the following morning. He did not know what to feel. He had accomplished the task he had set for himself, but he knew he would pay a price for it. He also thought about Sonny and how things change. When they were kids playing in a sandbox, Miguel would never have thought about burning Sonny alive. Miguel thought about those days, and missed the Sonny he knew then. Then he realized the Sonny he knew then had faded out of existence long ago, and the new Sonny was a Sonny the world was better off without. Miguel thought about this the rest of the day, and he thought about it deeply as he sat in a downtown bar at happy hour watching the six o'clock news report Julie's arrest and how her lawyer was already preparing an insanity defense. Miguel became so lost in thought about it as he crossed the street to the next bar, that he did not see the speeding pick-up coming toward him.

Later that night, as Miguel lay in his hospital bed waiting to fall asleep, he remembered the last time he saw his grandfather. They had finished their supper and were sitting on the old man's porch looking at the stars, puffing on a couple of cheap cigars, and listening to the coyotes yip in the distance.

"Miguel," said the old man.

"Yes, sir."

"The time has come for the final test."

"Tell me what it is and I will do it."

"Will you? Do not be certain until you have heard what it is."

"If you tell me I need to do it, I will do it."

"I want you to kill me."

Miguel was stunned. His initial reaction was to ask why, but the old man had taught him that to question the judgment of someone is a sign of disrespect. He knew the old man must have contemplated his death for some time and that the decision to die must have been well thought out. He did not want to see the old man go, but to protest would have been futile, because he knew the old man took great pride in keeping his word. If he said he would do something, he did it. For that reason, he rarely promised even trivial things.

Miguel flicked the ashes from his cigar and said, his voice cracking slightly, "I will do it."

"You do not weep," said the old man.

"You have taught me well."

"I have. That is true."

"How do you want to die?"

"How do you think I want to die?"

Miguel nodded slightly several times. "Of course. When?"

"Tomorrow night. After the tequila has left our bodies." The old man flicked the ashes from his cigar and spit on a scorpion he saw crawling across the porch. "This will be a hard task for you. It would be a hard task for anyone. I am proud that you accept it."

"The hardest part will be to wait for you to die the next day."

"That will not happen. I have spoken with the ancient gods and they will allow me to pass quietly in my sleep when I die in the dream."

Miguel nodded. "Why now?"

"I am over a hundred and twenty years old. I love this world more than I have ever loved anything else: women, rifles, knives, whores, cantinas, or even horses. But I want desperately to see the next. I want to be with my ancestors and the friends I have not seen in decades. I want to be with two of my wives again. The third can keep rotting in hell. Now that I have passed on my knowledge to a man I can respect, I can go to the next world in peace."

"Thank you for passing on your wisdom."

"Do not thank me until you are ready to go to the next

world and you have seen if that knowledge has helped you. Do you know why I have chosen this as a test for you?"

"I think so. If I can overcome the love I have developed for you, and I can kill you in the ancient way, I will have mastered myself and will be able to kill anyone."

"That is right."

Throughout the rest of the evening, Miguel thought constantly and deeply about his grandfather's chosen means of death. But he controlled his emotions tightly and did nothing that he did not do every other evening he had lived with his great-grandfather. That night, he visited the old man in his dreams, taking along a bottle of tequila with a rattlesnake coiled inside. He went to the side of his grandfather's bed, where he slept with the covers pulled over his head because of the cold night, and said, "Wake up, old man. We are not finished saying farewell."

The covers moved and his great-grandfather rose, but not as an old man. When he stood, he was a young man of twenty. They talked long that night as any two young men do about the things young men enjoy: women, guns, liquor, tobacco, and the accomplishments of which they were most proud. Miguel also spoke of the things he had decided he would accomplish in this life, and his great-grandfather gave him the benefit of his years and advised him on how to achieve his goals. In their shared dream, they fell asleep together with Miguel's head on his great-grandfather's chest.

They went about their usual chores quietly the next day, each thinking about the night to come and each speaking very little, each striving for control over his emotions. When evening came and they had finished supper, they went out to the porch, where they once again smoked while listening to the coyotes and talked about the stars. When the moon rose above the trees, the old man rose and went to bed. Miguel stayed on the porch until he heard snoring. He went into the cabin and gathered the maguey thorn, ololiuqui seeds, pulque liquor, copal, paper, and a cigarette lighter, and went out to a point several yards from the cabin, where he began the ceremony. When he was finished, he went to bed, and fell asleep thinking that would be the last time he would ever hear the old man snore.

In Miguel's dream, he was an Aztec priest in full ceremonial regalia standing atop the Great Temple in Tenochtitlán long before Cortez set foot on Aztec soil. A few puffy, white clouds skirted the horizon and a gentle breeze blew feeling good as it cooled the sweat on Miguel's skin. At the base of the temple, thousands gathered and gazed up at Miguel. Then a young man in a loincloth came out of the crowd and slowly, solemnly climbed the steps to the top. When he arrived, Miguel could see it was the young form of his great-grandfather. He looked Miguel in the eyes and said, "thank you." He then proceeded over to the altar, where he lay down spread eagle. Miguel tied down his wrists and ankles and from underneath the altar picked up an obsidian knife. He chanted a ceremonial prayer to the Aztec gods, and then, turning, looked down at his grandfather's eyes and for a moment thought that he could end this now and wake up. He then thought about how that would disappoint his great-grandfather, but put those thoughts out of his mind. He knew what the old man would advise in this case: to put aside all thoughts of anything or anyone else and do what you have to do. Miguel then touched the knife to his great-grandfather's skin just below the ribs to the side of the solar plexus, made a quick and deep incision while the man squirmed, reached up inside the chest, tore out his heart, and flung it into the sun.

4

Devil Star's Revenge

On one of the last warm days before winter blew into the Four Corners area, I was sitting at a table on a coffee shop's patio in Farmington, New Mexico, enjoying the feel of sunshine and a slight breeze on my face and sipping a hot pumpkin spice latte. Then the breeze shifted to behind me and the pungent stench of death filled my nostrils. I turned out of curiosity, thinking it must have been a dead skunk on the shoulder of the nearby street, but instead I saw a tall, weathered cowboy with sunken eyes staring at me from only a few feet away.

"Got a dollar?" he asked. His voice was raspy and deep. "I know it's a lot, but I need something to eat and I can't seem to get anything for less. The hunger's been getting the best of me."

He was obviously telling the truth. He must have been six foot six, but I doubt he weighed more than 175 pounds. I thought he must have been near death. He was pale and his skin clung to his bones, making him appear much older than he probably was. Something in his eyes, voice, and stance told me he was probably in his early thirties, making his physical state tragic instead of merely shocking. Even in the shade of his battered cowboy hat, I could tell that his pale blue eyes were rheumy and devoid of sparkle, which gave me a chill, because I had seen the same lifeless eyes in my relatives who had passed away soon afterwards. His sallow cheeks were covered in stubble, except for his upper lip, which sported the remains of a once bountiful moustache. He wore a red bandana and a dusty, ill-fitting but new shirt. His old-style jeans were baggy and rotting and covered slightly bowed legs and the tops of weathered cowboy boots.

I don't usually give money to panhandlers, suspecting that instead of spending it on food, they will spend it on meth or whatever chemical brought them to their condition. But all panhandlers I had seen previously looked like they had had a meal in the recent past. This poor bastard looked like he hadn't had a meal in years. Still, I had been tricked before.

"I don't normally carry cash on me," I said. "I put everything on my credit card. If you like, I'll buy you something to eat."

"Yes, please, sir. I haven't eaten in a long time."

"Take a seat."

"Thank y', sir."

"Is there anything particular you would like? Sandwich? Burrito?"

"Y'all eat burros now?"

I chuckled. "No, it's meat wrapped in a tortilla."

"Anything at all's fine by me. I'll even eat a burro."

"Wait here."

"Yes, sir."

I went inside and ordered two ham sandwiches, a piece of apple pie, and a cup of black coffee, all for him, at the counter. As I waited, I watched him. He leaned back in his chair, closed his eyes, and stretched his head back, enjoying the feel of the sun and wind on his face. He smiled. I have never seen a person in such bliss.

I took the food and coffee out to him and he wolfed them down. I asked a couple of questions while he ate, but either he did not hear me or he was ignoring me. Afterwards, from his shirt pocket he took out a small pouch, from which he took out some rolling papers and tobacco and started to roll a cigarette. I explained that smoking wasn't allowed there. He seemed puzzled, but he complied and put the materials back into his shirt pocket.

"Want anything else?" I asked.

"Naw, thank y'. I'd better not. I haven't eaten anything in a long time and I might hurt myself if I ate too much too soon. I'll wait awhile."

"Okay. Let me know when you want something else." He seemed relaxed and I didn't want to rush him off, so I started some small talk to pass the time. "You live around here?"

He half-way smiled. "No, I haven't lived around here in some time."

"What's your name?"

"Ezekiel Long. Call me Zeke." He reached out and we shook hands. His hand was cold and clammy. "You live here?"

"I live over in Aztec, about ten miles east of here."

"I know it. I used to court a gal over there."

"So, you're just passing through?"

"Yeah. Just passing through—sort of."

"Where are you headed?"

"The Apache reservation. I'm going to avenge myself on a medicine man...maybe his family, if he's not around anymore."

His straightforwardness and matter of fact tone took me back at least as much as the statement itself. I wasn't certain of what he might do if I tried to call the police or alert someone, so I kept my cool and tried to talk about it as dispassionately as he did.

"The Apache reservation is about seventy miles away. Are you going to walk the entire way?"

"I guess I will unless I can find myself a horse."

"There are some ranches along the river on the other side of Bloomfield. You might find one there."

"That's good to know. Thanks."

"That's a long way to go just to kill someone. I take it that he did something serious to you."

"You're damned right he did something serious to me. He did this." With that he removed his hat to show a huge scar where most of the skin from the top of his head had been removed roughly and violently. Then he took off his bandanna to reveal a huge cut stretching across his throat that had never healed properly but did not bleed. He tossed his hat and bandanna onto the table. "Those ain't the worst though. The worst was that he brought me back to life."

Then Zeke related a story that, months later, still gives me shivers and makes my skin crawl at night. I haven't slept with the light off since that day.

Zeke was born in 1886. From his earliest childhood, he remembered being in love with a girl of the same age named

Eliza, whom he saw at church every Sunday, and whose farther, Jeb Holloway, owned a neighboring ranch.

When Zeke was nineteen and his brother Malachi was eighteen, their dad gave them enough money to buy a hundred acres for their own ranch. They already had about fifty head of cattle each, and with Malachi already engaged to Amanda and Zeke courting Eliza, they believed they were set for life.

Because Zeke was planning to marry Eliza, he talked Malachi into buying a hundred acres that bordered onto both their dad's and Jeb Holloway's ranches. Zeke and Malachi did not buy the water rights that came with the land, because the owner wanted more than they could afford. Therefore, they struck a deal with Mr. Holloway to buy the rights from him for a lot less than they were worth, because Jeb was looking forward to having Zeke as a son-in-law and as a neighbor, where he could easily visit his future grandchildren. Zeke and Malachi named their new property the Long L Ranch.

Because of their savvy business deal, Zeke and Malachi saved a lot more money than they had expected. They decided to go into Farmington and celebrate at the Elk Horn Saloon by becoming very drunk.

The saloon was crowded when they arrived. Just after they ordered their second round, Zeke spotted a whore named Mariposa, who bore a striking resemblance to Eliza. All day Zeke had been day-dreaming about his upcoming wedding night, so he decided to pay for a night with Mariposa. He offered to pay for a whore for Mal, but Mal passed on the offer, saying he had the patience to wait for what he wanted.

"You shouldn't be having one either," said Mal. "You don't want to give Eliza any lasting surprises on your wedding night."

"Ahh, I don't know anyone who's caught anything from Mariposa yet. Besides, she's looking pretty good tonight...like a dream. I just want to get me a taste of that dream. I'm tired of waiting. I have been trying to bed Eliza almost since I've known her, but she keeps saving herself for marriage. Hell, Mal, we've been waiting for good things all our lives, and I just want a taste of things to come. You know, like a kid that swipes a bit of icing off a cake when his ma isn't watching."

"Zeke, don't be stupid," said Mal, grasping Zeke's forearm as he rose from his chair. But Zeke shook it off, walked up to Mariposa, put his arm around her waist, and led her upstairs to the second floor.

About a week later they met Jeb at the courthouse to pay for the water rights and draw up the papers.

When Jeb entered, he was furious. He walked up to Zeke, looked him in the eye, and said, "You son of a bitch! I just heard from Mike Higgins that he saw you take that whore Mariposa to one of the upstairs rooms last week. You ain't giving my daughter no sicknesses. To hell with you both! I'll never let you near my daughter again and I sure as hell won't sell you any water rights. You stay away from my ranch. I'll string you up if I ever see you on my ranch again."

"That ain't right," said Zeke. "We already struck a bargain."

"I ain't striking a bargain with you or any other whoring son of a bitch!"

Zeke took a swing at Jeb, but he was agile for any old man

and ducked the punch. He floored Zeke with a right cross. As Jeb turned and stormed out, Zeke shouted, "That ain't right, you old bastard! I'll take you to court. We've got to have those water rights."

Having those rights was critical to Zeke and Malachi. Without those rights, they wouldn't be able to get water for their ranch and it would be worthless.

They took the case to court in San Juan County and lost. They appealed and the next hearing was held in Santa Fe, several days ride across the Apache reservation to the east. Despite hiring the most expensive lawyer they find, they lost the case. They decided to sell the ranch for what they could. To drown their sorrows, they decided to get drunk at Rosa's Cantina near the city square.

At Rosa's, Zeke met a half-breed whore named Belle, who, after several whiskeys, he thought looked something like Eliza and who had the same long, dark hair as Eliza that he always loved to smell and feel draping across his face whenever he kissed her. Once again, Malachi tried to talk Zeke out of a foolish decision, but Zeke just brushed him off and said it wasn't right that he should never see Eliza again.

Zeke did not remember much of that night, except for foggy memories of pounding Belle hard, riding her as a stud does a mare, throwing her around the bed, and occasionally having sex on the floor and even on the windowsill—to the raucous amusement of passersby in the street below.

The next morning, Belle told Zeke he had been rough on her and that he would have to pay for her bruises. He could see that he had choked her at some point, because she had a ring of bruises around her neck where his hands had been. He tossed a dollar onto the bed in addition to what he owed, but before he left, he asked if she would like to come to Farmington with him.

"I wish I could," she said with sincere remorse, "but all my family is here and my mother is sick with consumption."

Zeke felt anger and frustration quickly rise within him. For a second he tried to restrain himself, but he felt it shoot out of him and he punched a wall, knocking a fist-sized hole in it and scaring Belle, before muttering "lyin' whore" under his breath and storming out.

On the return leg of their journey, Zeke and Malachi passed through the Apache reservation once again. They were talking about Malachi's upcoming wedding to his childhood sweetheart named Amanda, when they spotted in the distance a large herd of elk led by two large bulls, each with a fine set of antlers.

"Hell," said Zeke, "just one of those racks would look nice on my wall at home."

"Yeah, I'd like that too," said Malachi, "but I don't want to go hunting on Apache land. They spend most of the time starving, because the land is so worthless they can't grow anything. You shoot an elk and you're taking food out of their mouths. They're very protective about what's theirs. God help us if they were to catch us."

"Well, I want to get something out of this damned trip, even if it's only an elk rack and enough meat to get us to Farmington. They ain't going to catch us. It won't be too long until it's dark and then we can high-tail it west. No one will be able to track us at night."

Malachi had his doubts about not being caught, but he understood Zeke's frustration over their day in court and his desire to profit something from the long, arduous journey. Malachi trailed behind Zeke and kept a watchful eye out as they tracked the herd.

Shortly before sunset, Zeke and Malachi seized the opportunity and, firing simultaneously, brought down both bulls. As the herd bolted, Zeke fired at a cow bringing it down as well.

"What the hell are you doing, Zeke? We can't even pack the meat from the big bull alone on both our horses. What did you bring down the cow for?"

"Just for meanness, I guess. There are too damned many Apaches anyway."

They rode over to where the biggest bull had fallen and started butchering it.

Just as the sun started settling below the horizon, Malachi glimpsed movement at the top of a nearby rise between him and the setting sun. Spread out along the top of the rise were the silhouettes of twelve horses with riders. Above them hung the evening star, blazing like a silver lantern, throwing light onto the crimes of Zeke and Malachi.

Malachi put his hand on the handle of his Colt Peacemaker in his gun belt. "Zeke," he said to get his brother's attention.

Zeke looked up and saw the riders. He put his hand on his own Peacemaker.

The riders rode abreast slowly down the slope. As they approached, Malachi saw there were ten young Apache men with rifles and bandannas around their heads; a pretty young Apache woman with a shawl around her shoulders in the formation's center; and a stern, middle-aged man wearing a weathered Stetson with a single feather protruding from the band. He was short and stocky with broad shoulders, a square head surrounding a fearsome scowl, and black slits for eyes. Malachi recognized him.

"That's Devil Star," he said.

"Who?"

"Devil Star. They say he's a powerful medicine man that has been alive since creation and can bring the dead back to life.

"Bullshit," said Zeke.

"The girl is his daughter, Ela, and at least two of the men are his sons. I don't know about the others."

Although Zeke tried to keep his eyes on the men with rifles as they approached, he found it hard not to keep them on Ela. She bore some resemblance to Belle, and had long, dark hair, but Ela's was parted down the center of her scalp and woven into a long braid on each side. Something else reminded him of Eliza, though he could not put his finger on it. It might have been the way she held herself erect or the light in her eyes.

When the troop stopped, Devil Star said something loudly and angrily in Apache. Ela translated. She spoke surprisingly excellent English, just like Eliza, thought Zeke.

"My father says to leave the elk and ride off with your lives. We have not tracked this herd for a day only to have you steal the best of it from our reservation when our people are starving and dying of consumption. The only reason we do not kill you now is because we have already seen too much death among our own people. Go and tell all other white men there shall be no more stealing from the Apaches."

"Now, wait a minute," said Zeke, taking a step forward.

All the young Apaches aimed their rifles at Zeke's face and he stopped.

Devil Star said something else angrily and his daughter translated.

"My father says go now or we will skin you and leave you for the coyotes. We will do that to anyone who steals our elk. We will not warn you again."

Malachi and Zeke walked slowly backwards to their horses, mounted, and rode off, constantly checking behind them to make sure they weren't about to be shot in the back.

Just after dark, they made camp on a stream bank. All that night while they sat next to the campfire, Zeke cursed Devil Star and every Apache who ever lived. In the morning, they broke camp and started riding northwest toward Farmington. After a couple of hours, Zeke turned east.

"Where are you going?" asked Malachi.

"I'm going to get me something Apache. I ain't leaving this reservation empty-handed."

"You're too damned stupid for words—stubborn too. You heard what they'll do to the next white man they catch. And I don't want to be paying for your stupid mistakes again either."

"They ain't going to catch me or you. You go on back to Farmington. Take care of the ranch until I get there." With that, Zeke rode east, deeper into the reservation.

"Zeke! Zeke!" Mal shouted as Zeke rode off. "Damn you!

I ain't coming back to look for your carcass and I ain't gonna make my girl a widow before her time! Damn!"

Mal hesitated, trying to decide whether to ride after Zeke or to continue to the ranch. Finally, he chose to continue to the ranch. He had a new ranch and he would soon have a new wife. He had too much to lose to continue paying for Zeke's stupid mistakes. Besides, if he could talk to Eliza's dad for a little while without Zeke around, he might be able to work out a deal over the water rights.

Zeke was impetuous, but not completely stupid, thought Mal. He might ride a couple of miles and then see how alone he was and remember Devil Star's words and then head to Farmington. At least, that's what Mal hoped. Zeke was also stubborn; once he set his mind on something, he usually kept after it until he got it. Sometimes that could be a good quality, but it could be dangerous when combined with being impetuous. Mal sighed in resignation to the situation. He clicked his tongue twice to start his horse into a trot and headed home.

For two weeks Malachi waited for Zeke, checking the road to the southeast often and asking anyone coming from that direction if they had seen him. He spent a lot of time haggling with Mr. Holloway. Finally, they reached an agreement on the water rights, but the price wouldn't be as cheap as in the original deal and Zeke would have to keep his distance from Eliza or risk being shot.

One day while Malachi was having a beer at the Elk Horn, Zeke walked in and stood next to Malachi at the bar. Malachi was so excited to see his brother that he hugged him tightly and started to cry out of joy.

"Damn, Zeke, I thought you were gone for good. What happened? What did you bring back from the reservation?"

Zeke grinned evilly. "I didn't bring back nothing, except this smile."

Malachi looked worried. "What did you do?"

"I tracked those sons of bitches all the way over to that little Apache village they call Dulce. I stayed on a hilltop outside the town for several days waiting and watching to see what I could steal. Then one morning I saw Devil Star's daughter ride out of town headed west and I had an idea. I tracked her for a few hours and when she stopped at a creek to water her horse, I raped the shit out of her and left her for dead."

"You what? Are you crazy? Devil Star won't rest until he's killed both of us!"

"How the hell is he going to find us? He doesn't know us from any other white man."

"Why do you think I recognized him? I saw him and the girl over at that trading post near Huerfano Butte, when they came up here to trade for some sheep with the Navajo. I sold him some tobacco I happened to have. Devil Star had to have recognized me."

"Relax, will you? I left her at a creek in the middle of nowhere. They probably haven't found her yet."

"Are you sure she was dead?"

"Well, almost dead. She couldn't have lasted much longer. I beat her until she was almost dead. When I left her she was chanting something in Apache, but that's all she could do. She couldn't even get up off the ground."

"You had better pray to God that she died before they found her."

Several days later Malachi and Zeke came into town to buy supplies for the ranch. Malachi had brought the buckboard, but Zeke had ridden his horse so he could stay longer and take care of some business at the bank. About an hour after Malachi headed back to the ranch, Zeke bought a newspaper to read while he had something to eat at a hotel. In the newspaper he saw that the trading post near Huerfano Butte had been burned and its owners scalped and murdered. A band of Apaches had been seen in the area by ranchers and were suspected of being the culprits. Zeke reasoned that either Devil Star had not gotten the information about the Long brothers from the owners of the trading post and killed them out of anger, or he had gotten what he wanted and killed them to keep them from warning anyone. He decided to gamble on the latter.

Zeke paid and lit out on his horse to warn Malachi that Devil Star was on his way, but he was too late. On the trail back to the ranch, Zeke saw smoke rising from the road in the distance. He found that Devil Star and his band had already caught up to Malachi. They had turned the buckboard onto its side, tied Malachi spread-eagle to one of the wheels, cut him dozens of times, found the kerosene among the supplies Malachi had just bought, dowsed him in it, spun the wheel, and lit it. The wheel was barely moving when Zeke found the wagon, and Malachi was still barely alive, managing to whisper only "Amanda, Amanda" from between charred lips.

Zeke burst into tears and tried to comfort Malachi, but Malachi showed no sign that he knew that Zeke was there and screamed whenever Zeke touched him. Finally, Zeke pulled himself together long enough to draw his Peacemaker and send Malachi to his eternal rest. Zeke wept until well after dark before he could cut his brother free from the wheel, drape him across his horse, and head on to the ranch, Devil Star's band having stolen Malachi's horses.

The next day, Zeke took Malachi to the undertaker, so that he could seal the body in a casket before telling Malachi's fiancée and her family why Malachi couldn't make the wedding the following week and why she shouldn't have an open casket at the funeral. Zeke said that it broke his heart to hear her wailing as he rode away and that after a hundred years her voice still echoed in his mind. Once at his own home, Zeke filled his saddlebags with as much money and valuables as they could hold, and said farewell to his parents. After a hundred years, he could still hear them sobbing.

Zeke followed the La Plata river north for a few days into the mountains to a cabin he and Malachi used occasionally when hunting elk. His plan was to stay at the cabin for a night and make Durango a day or two later, where he could stay at a hotel until he could catch the next train east. He knew the Apaches were good trackers, but he hoped he had covered his tracks well enough that he could at least get a day or two jump on them, before they figured out the direction he was heading.

While he was asleep, just before dawn of the morning he was to depart for Durango, Zeke felt a heavy weight upon his chest and his arms pinned down on either side of the bed. He awoke to find Devil Star sitting upon his chest with a Bowie knife while two young Apaches held down his arms. He started to plead, but his pleas changed to screams and then gurgling as Devil Star grasped his hair, cut away his scalp, and sliced his throat long and deep.

A passing semi blew its horn and Zeke paused his story until it passed.

"The next thing I knew," said Zeke, "was that I awoke stretched out in a narrow box that smelled of pine. It took me a minute to realize what had happened. Instead of leaving me to rot in the cabin, Devil Star had dumped my carcass at the ranch where my ranch hands could find it and my family could bury it—just so he could bring me back to life once I was in the ground!"

"I screamed and pleaded with God for I don't know how long until finally I settled down and did nothing but try not to go crazy.

"I started to try to claw my way out once, but figured out that I would weaken the wood and the lid would collapse, paralyzing me under tons of dirt.

"You can imagine what it was like: eternal cold, darkness, silence, hunger, thirst, and frustration from not being able to move but very little. Aside from those, one of the worst torments was hearing something move. I knew that it was something burrowing along the walls of the coffin and that there was probably nothing I could do to keep it from burrowing in and doing what it would with whatever of my parts I could not reach. Worms were the worst. I could hear them tunneling through the wood, weakening it. Sometimes I thought I heard rats or gophers. Once I thought I heard something brushing against the outside and I figured it was a snake.

"Sometimes what was worse was when I would try to talk to the critters, and they would stop scratching or whatever and I was left in the black silence again, praying for whatever it was to come back so I could hear something again just for a second. I was damned if I heard something and feared it would burrow into the coffin with me, but then I was damned if I didn't hear anything and I would start pleading for something to come back just so I wouldn't be alone anymore.

"Worms were their own special torture. For a long time, I worried about them eating through the coffin and then eating into me. I fought them off as best I could for a long time, but they finally managed to burrow into me and started feeding on my feet where I could not reach. Then gradually they made their way up my body to my head and face no matter how much I fought. I could dig out the ones just under my skin that I could reach, but the others I could only suffer. I suppose the only reason they did not eat me completely away was because I was doomed to live forever and so my body kept healing and feeding them. The worst were the ones that managed to get behind my eyes. So long as the worms were feeding I could not sleep. Those that I could dig out became my only food, except now and then I would feel something like a bug running across my hands or face and if I caught it, I could choke it down.

"Sometimes water would start filling the coffin and I would think there had been a heavy rain that raised the water table. A few times it almost filled the coffin to the lid, leaving me only enough space to keep my lips and nose above its surface. Sometimes it got into my mouth and I would gag and choke until the water receded.

"Mostly, when there was nothing to distract me, I lay

there and wondered what was going on above ground with my family and with Eliza. I heard something digging to my left for a long time once and I guessed it was somone digging a grave for someone else in my family. I shouted and shouted and shouted, but there was never a response. After that I used to weep a lot thinking about how I could have been out if they had heard me.

"I remembered my life and wept and wept and wept. That was probably the worst torment I ever felt: having nothing to do but contemplate my wasted life and my miserable future, while imagining what life was like for my kin and friends as they lived to be old, watched the generations pass, and finally passed on themselves, for which I envied them.

"Finally, I got to thinking, daydreaming, about vengeance. That was all I could do: pray and dream about somehow escaping and taking vengeance. Finally, it came to me that Devil Star can live forever. Malachi had said that Devil Star was supposed to be hundreds of years old. After what he had done to me, that made perfect sense. Who wouldn't want to live forever so long as he could be free? But forever will be hell on Earth for him without his skin."

With that, he drew a new hunting knife from the back of his trousers.

"Where did you get that?" I asked.

"You would be surprised what you can get when people ain't looking."

"But how did you get out?"

"Yesterday, I felt the ground tremble and heard a dull roar and metal clanking and something scraping across my coffin lid. Then I heard some men yelling 'Stop! Stop!' and what sounded like shovels digging around me. Then somebody pried off the lid. I opened my eyes to see three men wearing orange vests and white helmets staring at my face. When I said, 'who the hell are you?' they dropped their tools and ran like jackrabbits.

"I crawled out of my grave and saw another fellow jump off and run from a huge yellow machine with a big yellow metal blade that must have moved the dirt off me. I looked around and saw I was in a pit. I saw a young fellow behind me. He was holding a shovel and was so scared that he was shaking. I asked him what that place was. He was trembling so much that he couldn't speak until I grabbed him by the collar and pulled him up to me real close and asked him again. He said something about it being a construction site for a *convenient* store. I asked him what a '*convenient*' was, but he just fainted dead away. I let him drop and started walking. I've been learning about this new Farmington since then."

Zeke rose from the table, put his hat and bandanna back on, and said, "Thanks for the grub and coffee, but I have me a medicine man to skin. See you around some time."

He started to amble off, but I spoke up. "It's none of my business, but if you skin Devil Star...if the police—if the sheriff catches you'll go to prison for life. For you that may be a very long time."

"They don't hang people any more?"

"Not in this state. They abolished the death penalty in 2009. Maybe you can start over. You've got a second chance. You've still got a young man's body—after you heal for a while, I guess. How old were you when you died?"

Zeke appeared somber and contemplative. "Thirty-four. I guess I lost a lot of weight in the coffin." Zeke looked over himself, muttering. "These were my best duds too...and my favorite hat and boots, except for the shirt. Mine was in shreds when I got out of my grave, so I had to steal this one. My clothes didn't last as well over the years as I did."

"You can have a whole new life, if you let Devil Star go."

I watched him until he was out of sight. I thought about calling the police to report a potential murderer, but what could they have done anyway? Even if the old man told them what he told me, to them he would have been just another crazy homeless guy who hadn't done anything they could arrest him for.

5

Shapeshifter

Late one October morning in the year 1601 outside a small town in the Jura Mountains northeast of Lyons, France, the cobbler Henri, a man well respected in the community for his intelligence and logic, was walking through a pasture straddling a low ridge on his way to his brother's farm to borrow a hammer. To pass the time on the long road, Henri was mulling over a conversation he had the previous evening with the mayor and several other friends as they sat around Henri's fireplace getting drunk until late into the night. For a moment Henri stopped and gazed at the faint sun trying to burn through the mists enshrouding the surrounding forest. He then looked at the narrow path ahead and shook his head as he muttered to himself, "It amazes me that such an intelligent man as the mayor would be so gullible as to believe that the world circles the sun."

As Henri continued up the crest of the ridge, he discerned a faint sound coming from down the slope to his right. After a few more steps he recognized the sound as a woman shouting. "Hmph," he muttered, "it must be the widow Beauchamp cursing her chickens again." As Henri walked a little farther he could clearly distinguish shouts of "Go away, you foul beast, go away!"

Fearing the widow might be in danger, Henri picked up a large branch lying under a nearby tree and, after three attempts, broke it over his knee to form a hefty club. He then picked up a large stone and started in the direction of the shouting. The closer he came to the widow's farm, the clearer the desperation of the widow's shouts became, and Henri's pace progressed from a walk into a trot into a run.

Charging down the slope Henri emerged from the mists into the bottom of a grassy valley. A short distance ahead was the widow's decaying farmhouse and beside it was the widow swinging a rusty sword at a scrawny wolf trying to get to an injured lamb behind the widow. Henri sprinted ahead, threw his stone, and shouted, "Go away, you old hellhound! Get out of here! The devil take you!"

Just as Henri shouted, "the devil", the stone struck the wall close to the wolf's head startling him. The wolf glanced at Henri charging from the side with a large club, then back at the widow with the rusty sword, and dashed from the farmhouse and down the valley.

Henri ran up to the widow and stopped, wheezing and panting. "Did you did you, whew, did you see that? He-he started at the devil's name. He must be must be a werewolf."

"I think it was the stone that scared him away," said the widow. "It certainly startled me."

"Non-nonsense. It had to be the devil's name. Sure, a stone might scare him a little, but he was terrified. He must be a werewolf."

"Well, maybe. You know more about these things than I do."

Along both sides of the valley Henri saw men carrying hay forks, clubs, and swords running toward the widow's house leaving the wolf nowhere to run but down the valley and into the town. Henri heard hoofbeats behind him and turned to find Pierre the blacksmith approaching on horseback at full gallop. Pierre reined in his mount next to Henri. "What is the matter? Why all the excitement?"

"We just chased off a werewolf. See! There he goes down the valley." Henri pointed ahead.

"Werewolf? A werewolf is a serious matter. Werewolves are being burned almost every day over in Franche-Comte. We can't let them spread into this province. We'll never get rid of them. They're worse than Protestants." Pierre reached down and took Henri by the arm. "Climb up. Let's go after him." With Henri clutching to his back, Pierre galloped down the valley toward the retreating wolf and shouted to the men coming down the slopes, "Get him! He's a werewolf! Werewolf!"

Within a minute the call of "Werewolf!" echoed throughout the valley. More men came running with whatever weapons were at hand. All headed for the lone wolf sprinting across the open pasture.

By the time the townspeople took up the cry, the wolf was already well down the main street. Surprised townspeople began shouting, "Wolf! Wolf!", and throwing anything handy to ward off the invading beast. In seconds the wolf ran headlong into a hail of cobblestones, sticks, pots, garbage, and farm tools coming from all sides but one, into which the wolf ran only to find himself in a dead end alley. The wolf stopped halfway down the alley and glanced around frightened. Around a corner to his right he heard a loud belch and turned to see the back of a small man urinating against a wall. The wolf heard the shouts and clatter of a mob converging on the alley. He glanced around the dead end again and spotted in the shadows at the far end a large barrel, behind which he could hide or make a last desperate stand. The wolf crept past the man and bounded the last few feet. Behind the barrel, the wolf found a large hole, evidently dug by dogs or children, leading underneath a wall. The wolf squeezed through and found himself behind a pile of hay inside a small stable. Looking around, he found no more openings and the only door locked. He lay down in the darkness behind the hay and waited.

Outside the wolf heard the commotion as the mob surged into the alley and found the small man fastening his belt. Several large men pinned him roughly against the very wall against which he had been urinating and shouted, "We have him! We have the werewolf! What do we do with him? What do we do?"

"Burn him! Burn the werewolf!" came a chorus from the back of the mob.

"No! Don't burn me! Mercy! I'm no werewolf!"

The entire mob took up the chant," Burn him! Burn the werewolf!"

"No! I'm no werewolf!"

"Then where is he?" a ragged man with rotting teeth and his calloused hand around the small man's throat asked menacingly. "We all saw him run in here."

"Yes, we did," shouted the mob.

"And you're the only one in here," said the man with rotting teeth.

"Burn the werewolf!" shouted the mob.

"I saw no wolf run in here," said the small man.

"That's what we would expect a werewolf to say," said the man with rotting teeth. "Get a rope and let's tie up the werewolf," he shouted to the mob.

"Burn the werewolf!" went up the cry.

"No, wait!" came a shout from the back of the crowd. "We have to make certain he's the werewolf."

The mob turned to see Pierre and Henri astride Pierre's sway-backed mare. Henri looked down upon the rabble and for a moment thought he knew what it must have been like to be Moses speaking down to the Israelites. "Werewolves can appear as anything. How do we know he didn't take on the form of a rat and is hiding in that barrel in the far corner? Let's make certain we know what we're doing before we burn anyone."

"Yes! Yes! I agree!" shouted the small man.

"Shut up," said the man with rotting teeth. "We'll hear your voice enough as you scream from the top of your pyre." He turned to Henri. "How do we make certain?"

Henri dismounted and brushed through the crowd to almost press his face against the small man's. "Say the Lord's Prayer." Henri turned to address the mob. "Werewolves can't say the Lord's prayer because they're servants of the devil and can't ask for forgiveness of their sins." He turned back around and stuck his face so close to the short man's that their noses almost touched. "Say the Lord's prayer."

The short man's lips quivered as he stammered, "Ou-ou-our F-Father, who art in heaven, hallowed be thy name—"

"In Latin! Or are you afraid to speak the language of the church?"

"P-Pater n-noster…"

Through a hole in the barn wall the wolf was watching the man tremble as the mob pressed closer to him waiting to see what would happen when he arrived at the words "forgive us our sins". Then the wolf heard footsteps approaching the doors, as the scent of a man grew stronger. The wolf backed into a dark corner and braced for a fight. He curled his lips back as he began to snarl. The wolf could hear the man stop, then give a wet, hacking cough, and spit. Three more steps and there was the soft clack of wood on wood as the man raised the latch. The door creaked and a beam of sunlight shot through and grew the more the door creaked.

When the door was wide open the man stepped into the darkness of the barn and paused to allow his eyes to adjust. Suddenly the wolf hit his knees at a dead run and sent him sprawling backwards into the sunlight. He rolled onto his stomach in time to see the wolf's hindquarters speeding down the street. "Wolf! Wolf! There's the wolf!" he shouted.

Again shouts of "Wolf! Wolf!" reverberated through the town and the wolf ran dodging vegetables, cobblestones, and cooking pans. The wolf rounded a corner and then another, ran past four more streets and found himself in the market in the town square. More vegetables flew at him. He bumped against the legs of a woman and sent her crashing into a cartful of turnips. Children ran after him throwing whatever was at hand. An old man swung at him with his walking stick and missed. A mongrel dog gave chase for a few seconds before a cabbage intended for the wolf hit him full in the muzzle. Several townspeople immediately fell upon him and pummeled him to death thinking they had caught a second wolf.

The crowd closed in from the left and right forcing the wolf straight ahead and up the steps of the church as a door opened and out stepped the priest to be knocked down by the wolf as he bolted inside.

"Quick! Quick! Close up the church!" several people shouted, "We have him now!"

Inside the wolf dashed down an aisle and stopped before the altar. He glanced around looking for an exit. Off to one side a door was slowly opening. The wolf ran ahead and hid in the shadows of the back row of the choir box. The wolf lay still and scanned the nave through the intricately carved choir screen.

A well-dressed, corpulent man entered from the door, dipped his fingers into a holy water font, made the sign of the cross and bowed, and ambled over to a pew, where he sat, then knelt, and began to pray. Although inside the church was quiet to the man on the pew, the wolf's ears could listen to the shouts outside as calls to lock the doors circled the building. Isolated from the outside world by thick stone walls, to the man the shouts seemed barely audible murmurs. To the wolf, though, the voices were clear. He picked up his ears on recognizing a voice just catching up to the mob.

"Pierre, have all the doors been bolted?"

"Yes, Henri, and there are men outside each one."

"Where is the priest? Has anyone seen the priest?"

"I am behind you, Henri."

"Oh. Was anyone inside when you left, father?"

"No, no one. In fact, no one has been in the church all morning."

"Pierre, are you certain no one went inside before the doors were shut?"

"Uh, yes-maybe-sort of-no one got past me-I think. Everyone was at the doors as soon as the werewolf ran inside-maybe even before that."

"Good, then we have him at last. You there, boy, run to the men at the other doors and tell them to get ready. Something may try to burst out and if it does, they should kill it. We'll rush in from here. You men in the back, bring as much wood as you can find and start a bonfire. Is everyone ready?"

A cheer went up from the mob. The man in the pew raised his head from his prayer, listened for a second, shrugged his shoulders, and went back to his prayer.

"In we go!" shouted Henri. The mob cheered again and pulled the doors open. Noise and light coursed through the nave as the mob surged down the aisles toward the altar, but on seeing the lone figure to the side, they converged on him.

The man stood and faced the mob. "What is going on here?"

Those leading the mob stopped and gasped. The rest pressed against the backs of the first and on recognizing the man, they likewise stopped and gasped. The crowd quieted and only whispers disturbed the silence of the church.

"What is going on here?" demanded the man again.

Henri stepped forward. On recognizing the man his jaw dropped and his eyes widened.

"Henri, what is going on here? What is this madness? Well?"

For a few seconds Henri struggled trying to reason out what was happening as the now curious throng pressed against his back straining their ears to find out what was happening. Then Henri's face relaxed as his eyes narrowed, he closed his mouth, and he began to nod as if he understood.

"So, you have taken on the guise of the mayor. What a foul creature you must be to imitate such an upright and honorable man."

"It's the werewolf!" shouted Pierre to the mob.

"Burn the werewolf!" replied the mob.

"Werewolf?" said the mayor. "Are you insane? I'm no werewolf."

"Burn the werewolf!" shouted the mob.

"Burn me? No. No!"

"Burn the werewolf!"

"B-be reasonable. How c-can I be a werewolf? You all know me." Fear began to overwhelm the mayor and he began to tremble and sweat.

"Burn the werewolf!"

"N-n-no. Be reasonable. Have mercy!"

"Say the Lord's prayer," said Henri.

"What? Why? I'm no werewolf!"

"Say the Lord's prayer!" shouted the mob.

"The Lord's prayer? Why?"

"He's stalling!" shouted someone in the back.

"He's hesitating, because he's a werewolf," said someone else.

"N-no! I'm not. I-I'm not. Be reasonable. Please!"

"Say the Lord's prayer!"

"Wh-what? Why? What's the Lord's prayer to do with this?"

"Burn the werewolf!"

"We've had enough of your stalling, werewolf. Shapeshifter!" said Henri. "Burn him!"

The crowd cheered, seized the mayor, and hoisted him kicking and screaming onto their shoulders. As they rushed him out the door to the waiting pyre, the uproar drowned out his voice as he tried to recite the few bits of the Lord's prayer that arose in his confused mind.

As the last of the mob shuffled through the entrance, closing the doors behind them, the glow of fire began playing on the outside of the windows to one side of the church. The roar of the crowd and the screams of the mayor grew with the intensity of the flames. The wolf watched the flickering glow for a few seconds, then rose, and walked out into the nave watching for movement and sniffing the air. The stink of man lingered, but, except for the smell of rats, the wolf could detect no other creatures. The wolf plodded over to the basin, where the mayor had dipped his fingers, rose, and lapped up the water as the screams of the mayor faded away and the scent of roasting flesh wafted in. The wolf searched through the front of the nave and around the altar for rats to eat, but fatigue weighed more heavily on him than hunger and he plodded back to the shadows of the choir box to pass into sleep as the glow from the flames and the tumult of the crowd faded away.

Just before dawn the wolf rose and went to the font for another drink. As he lapped, the nearby door opened. The wolf quietly slipped behind the nearest pew. He watched as a carpenter entered carrying several tools, laid them near the altar, and went back out the door. In a minute, the door opened again and the carpenter propped it open with a large stone. He fetched more tools, brought them in, and laid them with the first ones. The carpenter went back outside and returned carrying several boards on the shoulder between his face and the wolf. As he carried them past the pew, the wolf slipped out the door.

Outside, the smell of burned meat was strong. The moon had already set, but here and there a soft glow from fireplaces or from the lamps of early risers seeped onto the streets. Keeping to the shadows the wolf worked his way around the church to the remains of the pyre, which was now only dying embers. The wolf circled the pyre, but could not find a way through the coals to the remains of the mayor without burning his feet.

A groan came from behind the wolf and he turned. Three men and a woman were lying together asleep on the cobblestones. They stank of wine. One of them belched and rolled onto his side. The wolf watched for a few seconds and then plodded away. As he left the pyre, the wolf found several more groups of sleeping men and women, some groaning, some belching, some coughing, some snoring, but all stinking of wine.

The wolf picked his way through the streets staying in the shadows and being alert to the slightest sound, smell, and movement. Outside a building from which glowed several lamps, the wolf stopped to drink from a puddle. Just as he finished, the door in the building opened and Henri, Pierre, and three other men stumbled out yawning, stretching, and stinking of wine. The wolf slipped back into a dark corner and watched as they passed.

"Henri, has anyone found the mayor yet?" asked Pierre. "He wouldn't want to miss something as important as a werewolf burning in his town."

"No, no one has and I don't think anyone is going to either."

"Why is that?"

"Well, put yourself in the mayor's position. If you were an important man like him, wouldn't you be embarrassed if a werewolf assumed your shape? He was probably so ashamed that he slipped out of town when no one was looking."

"He's probably afraid too that we'll think he's in league with the devil, because the werewolf assumed his shape. Did he at least say good-bye to his wife and children?"

"No, I went to talk to her just after the burning and she said that the last time she saw him, he was going to the church to pray that God do something about the werewolves that have infested the area. The werewolf must have seen him on the way to church."

"Well, it looks like God has started answering the mayor's prayers already. You're a very intelligent man, Henri. I wish we had a mayor as clever as you."

"Yes," said the rest of the group patting Henri on the back, "absolutely, we need a mayor like you."

As the group turned a corner, the wolf came out of the shadows, sniffed the air, and walked the opposite way down the street as first light began to show the silhouette of the forest's edge a short distance ahead.

6

Wolfsheim

As he stood in the growing twilight with cold rain dripping from the brim of his hat, Drake was nervous about continuing into the Alpine village of Wolfsheim about a kilometer ahead. Unfortunately, the only way to find the answers to his questions was to inquire at every village in this area no matter how much wrath and hatred those questions aroused.

For this latest day of hitchhiking through the Bavarian Alps, the weather had been mostly cloudy with rain imminent. Within the last few hours, fog had settled onto the pastures and enveloped the evergreen-covered slopes surrounding Wolfsheim. From this distance, the village impressed Drake as straight out of the Brothers Grimm. White two-story houses with tile roofs and brown shutters had brown flower boxes with red flowers beneath each window. An inn stood across the main street from a small train station, which lay next to the highway. In the central square stood a white church with an onion-shaped dome atop its bell tower.

Drake needed a place for the night as well as to make the inquiries for his "thesis", as he described it to strangers. He would get dinner and a room at the inn and he would talk to the waitress, if no one else were in the inn's dining room. He would have to be subtler than in the last village, where he had inadvertently aroused such ire that he had thought for a moment that he might be given the German version of a lynching. He had no idea what that might entail, but he felt certain it would have been professional, efficient, and painful.

Drake looked up and down the two-lane highway weaving through the forest and saw not a car. Nor did he see a single vehicle or even a person on the streets of Wolfsheim. A light rain started just as Drake was watching the top rim of the sun descend below a peak through a small break in the clouds and the long mountain twilight began. Drake was weary from a day that had started early and that had gotten him only a few short rides, so that he had spent most of the day walking. He adjusted the straps on his backpack and started toward the town.

As Drake trudged through the darkening rain, he thought up a cover story and several responses that would extricate him from any verbal quagmire he could anticipate, as well as a series of subtle questions that would hopefully attain what he needed without angering anyone. He would make it a point to sit near the door this time and, as he walked down the main street, he watched for potential hiding places and escape routes back to the highway.

As Drake entered the dining room, he glanced around. It was empty except for the table second closest to the door. There sat an older gentleman talking to a middle-aged man and a young man of Drake's age. Each man bore a resemblance to the other two and each had one hand on the handle of a half-empty liter mug of beer. All three appeared to have lived good lives in the mountains, because they were in obviously robust health. Drake set down his pack, took off his hat and raincoat, and took a seat at the table closest to the door. In a minute, a dour waitress strode quickly up to Drake, who ordered a half-liter of beer and Jaegerschnitzel. After she brought Drake's beer and scurried off to check on the Jaegerschnitzel, Drake said to the youngest of the Bavarians, "Pardon me, but could you tell me if the rumors about wolves in this area are true?"

The three looked at Drake and then at each other with unspoken questions. "What rumors have you heard?" the oldest asked.

"That there are lots of wolves in the mountains and that they sometimes prey upon hitchhikers."

"There are a few mangy wolves in the mountains, but they are harmless, unless you are a poodle," said the old man. He and the other two laughed. "Most of the wolves were all hunted out long ago."

"But in the village down the road they say there have been disappearances—"

"True," said the middle-aged man, "but that is more a comment on our tragic times, when violence is pervasive. The police are investigating those disappearances, and I have no doubt that they will come up with a solution other than starving wolves." The three men laughed again. "You are American, right? You speak German very well, but you still have a trace of an accent. What's your name?"

"Drake Hauptmann."

"Ah, Hauptmann! A good German name! Is your family from Germany?"

"Yes, my great-grandfather came from Garmisch-Partenkirchen."

"Bavarian as well! I am Dieter Schultz and this is my father Dietrich and my son Dietl. What brings you to Germany, Drake?"

"I'm working on my Master's thesis in history." At this point Drake knew he had to start being cautious and he began choosing his words carefully. "Specifically, I am studying post-war, uh, that is, recent German history."

"So what is the subject of your thesis?"

Drake took a long draught of beer to take a moment to think. "Well, it's somewhat complex, but essentially it is about Bavaria in the late forties."

"Then it should be interesting," said Dietrich. "I lived here then. Those were hard times. But then stories about a phoenix rising from an ash-heap are always interesting."

"So, you are here to conduct research for your thesis," said Dieter. "What exactly is its subject then? The rebirth of Bavaria?"

"No, actually, I am focusing on, uh, plans that were, uh, never realized." Drake took another drink.

"Never realized? Then you are focusing on failures? What is the point of that? What is to be learned?"

Then Dietrich cautiously posed a question. "Or are you focusing on one failure...or the failure of one group...perhaps the failure of a political party?"

"Yes," Drake confessed, "I am focusing on the failure of one political party."

At that moment the door opened and in walked six more Bavarians, all young or early middle-aged, all strong and robust. When they saw the Schultz family, they greeted them, and then moved on to a large table on the opposite side of the dining room. Drake sighed with relief when he saw they didn't sit near the door.

Dieter became quite serious and fixed an unblinking gaze on Drake. "What exactly is the subject of your thesis?"

Drake became nervous. "Well, let me say first that for a long time I have been fascinated with not only history, but also with theology and different belief systems and, consequently, some time back, my love of German history and theology sort of...became intertwined and I became interested in...the occult. A couple of years ago, I found out that at the end of the Second World War there was a group of former soldiers that decided to fight on as guerrillas after the war was over hoping to one day restore the Third Reich. They called themselves 'Werewolves—"

"We know all that," said Dietrich, now visibly irritated and very solemn. "Go on. What is the subject of your thesis?"

"Well, my theory is that the Werewolves were more than just guerrillas—"

"My God," said Dieter, "don't say what I think you are going to say."

"Well, Hitler was very much into the occult and a lot of the emblems and practices of the Third Reich did were rooted very deeply in the occult. So, I believe that Hitler actually formed a group of real werewolves to carry on the war—"

"And you came snooping around here to find the werewolves! You are mad, boy! Yes, the few fanatics that remained did operate down here as the Werewolves, but any that remain are very tight-lipped about it. And they are still very serious about protecting their identities even decades later. So are their families and descendants. Asking the wrong questions may cause you to disappear"

"Like that Englishman!" blurted out Dietl.

"Be quiet!" said Dieter. "And why would you want to find real werewolves? Even if they existed, they would tear you into smaller bits than real wolves would."

Out of the corner of his eye, Drake noticed that the men at the far table had turned around and were now watching him very closely.

"What have you learned so far?" asked Dietrich, eyeing Drake.

"Very little."

"But you have learned something?" asked Dieter.

"No, no, not really."

"What do you know?" asked Dietl.

"Nothing, really. Just a lot of rumors in some of the other villages—"

"Like what?" asked Dietrich.

"Nothing really."

"Like what?"

"There are some rumors and stories, and some government records support this, that…during the war…Wolfsheim was a center of, uh, werewolf activity." Drake paused and tried to think of something else to say, but he knew he had already gotten in too deep.

"Were any names ever mentioned?" asked Dietrich sternly.

"None."

"Are you certain?"

"None. I swear!" For a moment Drake paused, sweating and glancing nervously around him at the Schultz family and the men at the far table. Almost everything he had told had been the truth, but he sensed strongly that no one believed him. "It's getting late," said Drake rising, putting on his hat and coat, and picking up his backpack. 'I must be moving on. I'll just catch a train and be out of here"

"The last train left an hour ago."

Drake laid some cash on the table to cover the beer. "Then I'll have to hitchhike."

"Be very careful on the highway," said Dietrich, glaring at Drake. "Some say there are wolves in the forest."

"Thanks. I'll be careful." Drake looked over the room again. Every man was still and staring menacingly at Drake. "Auf Wiedersehen," said Drake. Then he remembered that meant literally "Until we meet again." He didn't want that, but could not take it back.

"Auf Wiederschauen," said Dieter, using the customary Bavarian response.

Dieter's tone frightened Drake, who turned and exited.

Outside Drake found that the rain had stopped, the clouds were breaking up, and he could see a few stars and the moon. Drake debated with himself whether he should let a room at the inn, but he reasoned that the innkeeper would probably be a friend of Dietrich and his family, and Drake did not want Dietrich to know where he was sleeping. He would rather take his chances on the highway, where he could run, if necessary, and he could find a secluded spot to sleep.

When he was about fifty meters from the inn, Drake checked behind him to see if anyone was following. Dietl stood in front of the inn's entrance watching Drake. He did not move. He only stood and stared. After another ten meters, Drake checked again and Dietl was still staring. Drake checked about every ten meters and Dietl continued to stare.

At that moment a black Audi pulled up with its driver's door alongside Drake. A tall, wizened Catholic priest sat behind the wheel and was the only occupant. The man appeared well over eighty, and weighed no more than 150 lbs. Underneath his frock, Drake guessed the priest resembled the lanky Christ seen on many crucifixes. The priest rolled down his window and asked, "Was there no room at the inn?"

"I did not ask. I felt uneasy there, and decided I would rather take my chances at the next village." Drake nodded in the direction of the next village along the highway.

"But that is so far and the weather tonight will be awful. You would have to hitchhike tonight because the last train has already left. Come. I have a small room in the church you can use. It has only a cot, but that is better than sleeping in the forest, especially on a rainy night. I even have an extra bottle of communion wine that I can let you have."

Drake mulled over his options before replying, "okay."

The priest opened the passenger's door and Drake ran around and hopped in, tossing his backpack into the rear seat next to the Father's communion kit. As Drake closed the door, he asked, "What's your name?"

"Father Hoffmann."

Drake shook the father's hand and introduced himself.

"So, what brings you to Wolfsheim?"

Drake did not want to lie to a priest. As the priest started down the street, Drake told his story as diplomatically as he could while watching Dietl continually staring at him.

"Does Dietl frighten you?" asked Father Hoffmann.

Drake shook his head. "Not really."

Father Hoffmann smiled. "Dietl is a little peculiar. I can understand why you would be uneasy staying in the inn his grandfather owns."

Drake silently thanked his lucky stars that he had made the right decision.

When they arrived at the church and Father Hoffman turned off the engine, he said, "Yes, here your thesis would certainly stir up many old feelings that are perhaps best left dormant." The Father shook his head as if resigning himself to something and said, "Come inside."

Both Father Hoffmann and Drake were silent as they went up to the church doors and entered. After they were inside, Drake followed Father Hoffmann through the church. Neither said a word. When they reached a small office in the back, Father Hoffmann set his communion kit on his desk and pointed to a door. "Your cot is in that storage room as well as a few blankets and a small pillow. In the morning, leave everything as it is and I will wash it. You may sleep in this office. You will find a toilet through that door," he said, pointing to another door behind his desk. He reached over to a cabinet and pulled out a bottle of red wine, a glass, and a corkscrew. "And here is the wine I promised."

"I sense that I have said something that disturbs you, Father."

"As I said, your thesis will arouse many strong emotions

here. That includes mine." Father Hoffmann took out the wine decanter from his communion kit and began filling it from a bottle on a rack near his desk.

"I am guessing that you lived here during the war?"

"Yes. I was thirty years old when the war ended. I had been a pastor here for only a short while when the first werewolves appeared."

"Did you ever see anything supernatural after they arrived?"

"I am a priest. In a sense, you could say that everything I do touches on the supernatural and that I see the supernatural in everything."

"Yes, but what I meant was—"

"I know what you meant. What I meant was that the world is as nebulous as the mists that surround this church tonight."

Drake was surprised by how quickly the pastor's tone had changed to rudeness verging on hostility. He looked out a window next to the pastor's desk. The streets were well lit by the town's streetlights and Drake could see Dietl standing next to the entrance to a dark alley across the street. Dietl was staring at Drake and continued to stare at Drake for several seconds before walking back toward the inn and disappearing around a corner.

"Dietl is outside watching us," said Drake.

"That is not good for you. His grandfather is perhaps the most fervent and most paranoid Nazi in this town. He would personally murder every Jew, Frenchman, and Russian alive today, if it would bring back the Reich." Father Hoffmann looked Drake straight in the eyes. "He would even murder Americans."

Just then a wolf howled. It sounded as if it were nearby, perhaps as near as the inn and definitely from that direction.

"Do not be frightened," said Father Hoffmann. "A wolf must have wandered into the square."

"Who said I was frightened? I find their howling beautiful. That is one of the many things that fascinate me about them. I grew up in an area of the Rocky Mountains where wolves are being reintroduced. Many times I have fallen asleep listening to their songs."

"Perhaps you have a wolven heart."

"Perhaps."

After the pastor finished filling his wine decanter, he took some wafers from a box on a shelf and placed them in the communion kit before closing it and setting it aside.

"Isn't it a bit late to come to the church just to refill your kit?"

"No, not at all. I had to give the last rites to a parishioner who lives—lived down the valley and thought I would refill everything before going home."

"I'm sorry."

"Why should you be sorry? It was her time to go."

"What did she die of?"

Father Hoffmann smiled a little as he closed his kit. "I hadn't realized the irony of it until now. She was apparently killed by a wolf."

"That is ironic." Drake thought for a moment. "You said, 'apparently'?"

"As I said, it is a nebulous world. Things are not always

what they seem. It was most definitely a wild animal of some type. But no one saw the attack and her throat was injured so she could tell no one what had happened before she passed away."

"Could it have been—"

"A werewolf? Who knows? Do you believe in werewolves?"

"Yes. Shakespeare said, 'there are more things in heaven and earth than are dreamt of in your philosophy'."

"Shakespeare must have been very astute."

"Is there another window somewhere that I can use to watch outside? I think all the windows I saw were stained glass."

"You did not notice that there are clear windows in the main entrance doors?"

"Oh, that's true! They are clear, aren't they?"

"I fear you will not get much sleep tonight, if you keep watching the street."

"I may have to if I want to survive the night."

"You sound as if you were trapped."

"I feel trapped. I feel like a wolf in a trap and I hear the hunters approaching."

Just then several wolves howled together. They were not far away.

Drake ran through the church to the main entrance and peeked out the windows. He saw the three men of the Schultz family loitering in the shadows at the entrance of an alley across the street and watching the church entrance. Drake glanced to the other side of the church and saw the other six men from the inn walking down the sidewalk, one dropping out of the group now and then to stop and start watching the church entrance.

Father Hoffmann came out of his office and walked up to Drake. "Is anyone out there?"

"Yes. I see several men. They are surrounding the church. Can we call the police?"

"It would do no good. Dietl's father is the Chief of Police."

"This gets better and better. Would you talk to them? Tell them I meant no harm?"

Father Hoffmann paused, thinking for a moment. "Yes. I will do that." He stepped outside and walked over to the Schultz family, who were gathered on a street corner. He spoke with them for a few minutes, and then Dieter Schultz waved to the others, summoning them over. When all nine had gathered, Father Hoffmann began speaking at length. Occasionally, someone would interrupt, but Father Hoffmann continued. Drake opened the door a little and tried to hear their conversation, but they were too far off and the wind in the trees was a little too high for Drake to discern most of their words. He caught only "wolves", "tradition", "the past", "murder", and a few prepositions. After about ten minutes, the Schultzes and their friends started going back to the inn, a few looking back at the church every now and then as they walked. In a minute, they had all disappeared around a corner, and Father Hoffmann was walking back to the church.

As the pastor entered the church, Drake asked, "they are gone?"

"They are gone."

"Thank you very much, Father. What did you say to them?"

"I simply appealed to their sense of reason. They are all good men at heart. I reassured them that you know nothing about Hitler's Werewolves and that whatever thesis you write would most likely go no farther than to the half-witted professor who assigned it. Most people believe the entire concept of a werewolf is preposterous anyway, and certainly any scholar worth his salt would look at your thesis as good only to line the floor of his birdcage."

Drake was dismayed at the pastor's argument. "Well, that is not the argument I would have chosen, but it worked. That is the only thing important now."

Father Hoffmann smiled. "Do not be hurt by what I said about your thesis. I am sure it will be a fine thesis, but to get them to leave, I had to say something that was logical and apparently true, even though it might not have been entirely true or even what I believe."

Drake let out a sigh of relief. "Thank you, Father."

"Now, how about we open that bottle of wine in celebration?"

"Certainly. I think I could use a drink now. I will go get it." Drake went into the back office for a moment, but when he returned with the opened bottle and two glasses, he did not see Father Hoffmann.

Drake walked up the center aisle and called for him, but he could not be found. He walked toward the doors, thinking Father Hoffmann must have stepped outside, but heard something snarling on the right. Drake froze, listening carefully. From behind the last pew came a large wolf, fangs bared, growling. The wolf crept forward with his head low-ered, ready to pounce. Drake slowly set the glasses on the floor, trying not to make any sudden movement or noise. He rose a little and crouched, holding the open wine bottle by the neck, its contents gurgling as they spilled onto the floor. He suddenly understood what had happened and said to the wolf, "Wait. Do not do this, Fath—"

The wolf sprung at Drake's throat. Drake quickly raised the wine bottle to crush the wolf's skull, but a hail of shots came from the entrance, splinters flew from the nearby pews, and Drake heard glass breaking behind him. The wolf fell onto the floor a meter in front of Drake and slid up against his feet. Drake raised his face to the doors, and saw the Schultzes standing there with smoking Glocks in their fists.

"This is why it is not good to snoop into the past," said Dieter, changing clips. Dietrich and Dietl changed clips as well, and the three walked up to Drake. They all looked at the body, which was now the naked body of Father Hoffmann, pierced with over a dozen bullet holes. "Are you okay?" asked Dieter.

"Yeah," said Drake. "Sure." Drake held the bottle upright and saw that a little wine remained. He chugged it down. "I'll be okay."

"We had always suspected that Father Hoffmann was the last of the Wolfsheim Werewolves, but we were never cer-tain. That is why we did our best to scare you off and that is why we sent Dietl out to watch and make certain you got to the highway safely. We knew Father Hoffmann would be re-turning soon. When Dietl told us that Father Hoffmann had driven you to the church, we thought that if he saw us standing outside the church, he would leave you alone."

"But you left."

"We only retreated farther back into the shadows, so that he could not see us. The rest of our group is still outside, watching the back doors and windows. We had to make him think we were gone, so that he would drop his guard. As soon as your faces left the windows, we moved up to peek inside."

"But I heard wolves outside—"

"Like I said earlier, a pack comes down periodically to raid our trash cans and pets. It was coincidence, but that is all."

"Your nerves must be frayed," said Dietrich. "Come. You may stay at my inn at no charge."

Drake hesitated in answering.

"Did Father Hoffmann tell you I was a werewolf?"

"He alluded to that."

Dietrich chuckled a little. "I was in the army, but I served on the eastern front, and spent most of the war and a few years afterwards as a guest of the Russians. Father Hoffmann may have exaggerated things so that you would feel safe with him. Now, would you like that room? And I believe that you never got that Jaegerschnitzel you ordered."

"Yes, I would like both very much, but I am too tense to relax right now. I think I will go for a walk first."

"Very well. We will be looking for you at the inn in a while. We have to clean up here first."

"Thank you. Auf Wiedersehen."

"Auf Wiederschauen," said Dietrich.

"Auf Wiederschauen," said Dieter and Dietl.

After Drake left the church he headed for the nearest edge

of town and found a trail that led into the mountains. The clouds and mist were dissipating and a gibbous moon gave the landscape a pale wash. Drake looked around and saw no one watching. He moved off the trail and into the black shadow of an evergreen. He looked back at the lights of the town. He could see police cars arriving at the church.

"What a shame," he said to himself. "I find one of the last remaining werewolves, and he is gunned down before my eyes. Oh, well. Maybe there will be more in the villages up the road." Drake heard his stomach growl and rubbed it. "I need to find something to eat and then to find some company I can relax with. I wonder if I can find that pack Dietrich mentioned." Drake removed his clothes, changed into a wolf, and loped along the trail into the mountains.

7

Hitchhikers

Colette and I had intended to leave Santa Fe and drive to the Grand Canyon on the morning after our wedding, but her brother Anatole's flight from France had been delayed by weather and he did not arrive until noon of that day. He lived in Lyon with their parents, therefore being able to see him in person was a rare occasion for her. We delayed our departure until late afternoon, so that I could meet him and the three of us could spend as much time together as possible. Anatole turned out to be as charming and intelligent as Colette had told me. Unfortunately, our late departure opened us up to a bizarre night I could never have foreseen.

We had had a reservation for a suite at the Bright Angel Lodge in Grand Canyon Village for months, and the rate being somewhat expensive and reservations hard to come by, we did not want to miss a night there. Normally, I would take I-40, an easy drive of seven and a half hours, but I had promised my grandfather in Farmington that I would bring Colette by and introduce her to my grandmother who was under hospice care. That meant we had to take US-550 to Farmington, and then US-64 and US-160 on across the Navajo reservation: a total of roughly eight hours, not including the time we would spend with my grandparents.

Because she tends to fall asleep earlier than I do, Colette drove first. We spent a few pleasant hours chatting with my grandparents, who, Colette said, were very much like her grandparents in Lyon. On departing, Grandma kissed us both and said she hoped that she would be around to see us again on our return. Collette's eyes and mine began to water and we promised to hurry back.

We drove on another forty miles before arriving in Shiprock, just inside the reservation, shortly after a brilliant vermillion and scarlet sunset. There we had a quick dinner and bathroom break before changing drivers and pushing on. We drove as fast as we dared, considering that we were traveling along a long, remote stretch of highway in unfamiliar territory and were already tired.

To say the reservation is sparsely populated is a gross understatement. The Navajo seem to enjoy their solitude and privacy and, although many do live in the few communities in the area, away from those their small homesteads are usually at least a few to several miles apart over rolling desert where the only light at night is from the moon, the thousands of stars sparkling intensely through crystal clear skies, and occasionally from a light from a distant farmhouse. That summer night was warm, clear, and moonless. We rode with the windows down to feel the desert air and to smell the aroma of wildflowers and the land.

We were several miles past the tiny village of Teec Nos Pos, traversing a stretch in which we had seen no signs of humanity, including any other cars, for maybe half an hour, when we spotted two young Navajo girls walking on the shoulder of the road. They had no flashlights or lanterns, and we noticed them only when their backs appeared suddenly in our headlights.

"My God, what are they doing out here in the middle of nowhere?" asked Colette.

"I have no clue," I said.

"Do you think we should offer them a lift? How far is it to the next town?"

"When I checked the map last, the next town of any size was Kayenta, and that's maybe seventy miles away still."

"Let's help them."

"Okay, just this once. I don't normally pick up hitchhikers, but these two appear harmless."

"Maybe their car broke down. God knows when the police might be out here, the last ones we saw were maybe fifty miles back."

I pulled over and backed up to within a few yards of the girls as Collette rolled down her window. The girls did not hurry or even pick up their pace. They walked up to Colette and looked at her with emotionless faces. The oldest girl was maybe sixteen and the younger ten. Both had long hair and wore jeans and denim blouses with silver and turquoise bracelets.

"Would you like a lift?" asked Colette.

"Sure," said the oldest. She opened the rear passenger door and the two quietly climbed inside and sat with their hands in their laps looking straight ahead through the windshield as if watching something in the distance.

"Where are you headed?" Colette asked.

"I'll show you where you can let us out," said the oldest.

"Okay," said Colette, somewhat nonplussed by the girl's abruptness.

"Did your car break down? Do you need us to call the police?" I asked.

"No," she replied.

"Do you live near here?"

"No."

"Do you need water or food? It's a long way from the nearest store or anything for that matter."

"No."

"Well, let us know if you need anything," said Colette.

"Okay."

"Can I ask your names?"

"I'm Mary. She's Maria."

"I'm Colette and this is my new husband Dean." Colette grinned, expecting congratulations and best wishes, but she received only silence, not even a half-hearted smile.

We drove on for about twenty minutes in almost total silence, except for Colette occasionally reading to me one of her friends' texts from her phone whenever we had reception, which was intermittent at best.

Out of curiosity, I watched the girls in the rearview mirror whenever I could. I noticed that Colette was doing the same in the vanity mirror.

The girls were as stone-faced, silent, and unemotional as any wizened old woman I had ever seen. For the first fifteen minutes, they sat still with their hands in their laps, gazing into the night ahead, their eyes moving little except to glance occasionally at me or Colette with disinterest.

Suddenly and in unison they snapped their faces to the right and watched something in the darkness as we passed it and left it behind. I looked in the rearview and as best I could out the windows, but saw nothing. They turned around in their seats and watched it out the back window for over a minute, speaking quietly and seriously to each other in Navajo. They turned back around in their seats and Mary asked Maria a question, to which Maria snapped back an answer as if annoyed. Then together they looked at the rearview mirror and stared into my eyes, which made me uneasy. I glanced at Colette and saw that she was watching them with curiosity in the vanity mirror. I turned my eyes back to the road. They said nothing else for several minutes and gazed intently into the darkness ahead.

Then Maria asked Mary a question, and they began to sniff the air. I sniffed quietly, trying not to draw their attention, but could smell nothing unusual. Then they both peered into the darkness as if searching for something. They did not look simultaneously in one direction as before, but independently and in as many directions as they could as quickly as they could, as if they were sparrows watching for predators. Then they sniffed the air again, said something to each other, and returned to quietly gazing ahead into the darkness after staring at my eyes in the mirror and making me uncomfortable. I turned my eyes again to look at Colette, who was still watching them in the vanity mirror. Colette looked at me and appeared bewildered, as if she wanted to ask, "*What have we done?*"

She turned to look at our passengers. "So, are you ladies sisters?"

Colette was doing the same thing she always did when something made her nervous: she was investigating to determine whether her fears were justified.

Mary said something to Maria. "Sort of," answered Maria.

"If you live out here, you must have a long bus ride to school."

"Grandmother teaches us."

"Oh. What do you want to be when you grow up? Do you want to move to the big city?"

"We will raise sheep as we do now."

"I see. Sheepherding is a good profession...I guess." Colette looked puzzled. "There must be a lot to learn about sheepherding. Does your grandmother teach you a lot about being shepherds? Is she a veterinarian or a biologist?"

"Grandfather teaches us to be shepherds."

"What does your grandmother teach you to be?"

"Witches."

Colette and I looked at each other in surprise. "I'm sorry," said Colette, "did you say 'witches'?"

"We're witches."

"I see," Colette said, trying to be nonchalant, "I teach world history at Santa Fe High, where Dean teaches French."

Mary and Maria said nothing and continued staring ahead.

"Well, if you will excuse me, I think I just received a

message on my iPhone." As Colette turned to the front, she glanced at me with a look of fright that I had never seen in her before. "Dean, we need to do something," she whispered in French. We always spoke French when we did not want others to hear what we were saying.

"About what?" I replied. "Are you scared of witches? Are you afraid they are going to turn you into a newt?" I smiled at the absurdity.

"You don't understand." She picked up her iPhone. She typed out a message in English and showed it to me. It was to my sister Beth in Albuquerque. It read: "Picked up two scary, young Navajo girls, witches, named Mary and Maria between Teec Nos Pos and Kayenta. If you do not hear from us tomorrow morning, send police. Kayenta still ahead."

"Honey, I think you're being silly," I said. "They're harmless."

"No, no, you don't understand. My family is from near Lyon—"

"Okay," I said. I hated seeing her frightened and wanted to calm her down immediately. "It won't do any harm. I don't want you to ever be afraid."

Colette nodded and sent the message. "*Merde*," she said under her breath.

"What?" I asked.

"It didn't transmit. I have no signal."

I could tell Colette was still worrying by the way her brow furrowed and her eyes were moist as if she were about to cry. She began drumming her fingers in her lap. I wanted to reassure her that the girls were harmless, but after thinking about it for a second, I had to admit to myself that I didn't know what they were carrying in their pockets and we had our backs to them. I had opened us up to possible danger by being too kind and by being too willing to give Colette anything she wanted that day. I started watching them in the mirror as often as I could, but every time I glanced in the mirror at them, both had their eyes fixed on mine.

Mary started to chant something softly in Navajo. Then Maria joined her. It had a primitive, throbbing beat. In my mind's eye, I could visualize the song being sung around a campfire a thousand years ago to the accompaniment of animal-skin drums, crude flutes, and gourds used as rattles while the eyes of animals in the surrounding brush glowed with reflected firelight. Colette fidgeted in her seat. The girls kept their gaze fixed on my eyes in the mirror.

Something about their stare unnerved me. At first I thought it was animalistic, but then I realized that it was not the stare of an animal, but of humans that had overcome animals and heat and storms and famine and thirst and savage, calculating enemies to become a people with a wizened, hardened soul, whose silence was their primary means of protecting the accumulated secret wisdom that had defended them against millennia of adversity.

"Stop at the road on the right," said Mary.

A minute later, a dirt road appeared on the right. I stopped. Except for starlight and our headlights, the night was black. I did not see a light in any direction.

Mary and Maria rolled down their windows and extended their heads out and stayed very still as if listening, staring out into the primordial darkness.

"Are you getting out?" I asked.

"Shh," said Maria. Neither moved. They began sniffing again, first Mary, and then Maria. Maria said something softly to Mary, who replied softly. They pulled their heads back inside. "Not here," said Maria. "There are skinwalkers here. Go to the next road."

Colette and I stared at each other in disbelief for a second. "*Skinwalkers?*" Colette said in French.

"You call them *shapeshifters*," I whispered to Colette in French.

Colette's left hand began to tremble as her eyes widened and started to tear up. The sudden and obvious terror that descended upon her surprised me.

I looked at Maria in the rearview mirror. "Certainly," I replied, tongue firmly in my cheek. "I'm no fan of skinwalkers either."

Several minutes later we came to another dirt road on the right. I stopped.

Mary and Maria repeated the process of searching the night, listening, and sniffing. Maria opened her door and walked down the side road and into the blackness.

"Go to the next road," said Mary.

"What about Maria?" I asked.

"She can take care of herself."

"Are you sure?"

"Yes." Mary glowered at me.

I looked at Colette in disbelief. "What can we do?" I asked in French.

Her face became stern and she replied in French. "Go. We are rid of one."

I had never seen her so cold-hearted. I pulled onto the highway and sped ahead.

"I don't understand you," I continued in French. "Why do you hate these girls so much? They're probably into some harmless, Wiccan-type stuff with the crystals and incense and New Age music in the background while they try to make love potions and crap. Yeah, they're creepy, but maybe that's just them."

"Do you know this woman you married? I'm from Lyon. I studied history in Lyon. Three hundred years ago in Lyon they burned witches and shapeshifters. I studied those burnings. Yes, some were innocent, but others were not. I believe many of those burned were evil people. No, I do not believe they had magic powers or flew about on broomsticks or changed into wolves or bats or whatever. But it doesn't matter what we believe; all that matters is what they believe, because they will act on those beliefs. In reality, witches couldn't use herbs to change people into animals, but they could use them to poison or drug other people. Shapeshifters were probably what we call "serial killers". To the uneducated, the mangled remains a serial killer leaves behind probably resembled the remains left by a wolf. Genuine witches and sorcerers were probably just evil people and were probably guilty of a lot of things that illiterate, superstitious peasants could understand only as magic. Just because someone was burned at the stake doesn't mean that they were innocent. We don't know these *witches*; we don't know what they can or will do."

"You were okay with picking them up."

"They were just young girls then. Now they are witches."

With that I shut up and drove on in silence. I did not want to argue.

We drove several miles before another dirt road appeared on the right.

"Here," said Mary.

I pulled over and she got out of the car. She walked down the dirt road without saying a word and never looked back.

I pulled back onto the highway while Colette repeated over and over, "Thank you, God. Thank you, God."

"We are not coming back this way," I said.

"That's right. We're not." She breathed a sigh of relief and leaned her head back onto the head rest and closed her eyes.

I leaned my head back on my headrest and exhaled slowly. The tension and nervousness were draining from me and I wished I had a beer to relax me. The air was growing cooler, so I rolled up my window. For the next several miles, I drove on looking at the wind rustle the bushes to either side of the road, trying to find a radio station that played music I like, and trying to reason out where Mary and Maria were going. By that time, Colette had dozed off and was probably dreaming of the Grand Canyon.

I noticed a few bright stars above the headlights. I looked out the side window and I could see the stars of Scorpio to the south shining far more brilliantly than the hundreds of others. Just as I turned my face back to the road ahead five coyotes ran out of the brush to the right. I slammed on the brakes, but I hit the fifth one and I heard a series of thumps as he passed under the car. "Shit!" I said.

Colette woke suddenly and asked, "What happened?"

We stopped and I looked in the rearview mirror. "We hit a coyote. I don't see him on the road behind us. He may be trapped under the car. I'll get out and look. I don't want him to get tangled up in something like a brake or gas line and then we're stuck in the middle of the desert."

Colette laid her hand upon my arm and said, "Be careful."

I smiled, trying to reassure her. "I have been around coyotes all my life. There's nothing to worry about."

I grabbed the flashlight from the glove compartment, got out of the car, and, hearing a pitiful whine, left the door open, and hurried to the rear bumper. A couple of feet behind the car a coyote lay on the asphalt. He was panting fast and lifted his head for a moment to look at me, as if asking, "What have you done?" He lay his head back down, and as he continued to pant heavily, his body began to lengthen, his fur withdrew into his skin, and he morphed into a young, naked Navajo boy. The boy raised his head and tried to say something, but he was too weak. His head fell back to the pavement. He twitched and lay still, staring across the road and into the desert night.

I heard something growling behind me. I turned to find the other four coyotes at the far edge of the road staring at me. All were growling.

"*Merde alors*," I heard Collette say through her open window. She saw them too. "*Vite! Vite! Allons-y!*"

They lunged forward as I sprinted to my door. Just as I reached it the lead coyote leapt at my throat. I hit him with the flashlight. He yelped and fell backwards. I slammed the door shut just before the other three coyotes lunged. They slammed against it in succession, falling to the pavement, then leapt up and tried to break through the glass to reach me, but only fell back snarling, growling, and gnashing their canines.

I gunned the engine and was up to seventy in a few seconds. In the side view mirror I saw a coyote and the boy lying on the asphalt while the other three coyotes pursued us for several yards. I checked the road ahead and then re-checked the rearview. There were two naked teen-aged boys lying on the pavement and three others standing, watching us drive off.

Colette turned to look out the rear window. Her eyes widened as she realized what was happening and stark terror enveloped her face. "Go! Go!" she said.

"I'm going! I'm going! I'm not stopping for anything until we reach Bright Angel."

The rest of the way to the Grand Canyon, we shivered and Colette snuggled into me tighter every time the headlight beams were caught in the eyes of some creature lurking in the bushes along the highway. Once in our room at the Lodge, we did not sleep until the sun rose and the only remnants of the darkness were the forest shadows.

On our return trip, we drove well to the north of the reservation and back into Farmington via Mancos and Hesperus. We spent a pleasant day with my grandparents, who told us that stories of experiences such as ours are not uncommon in that area. Though we occasionally go back to Farmington to visit Grandpa, who now lives alone, we seldom go west of there, and we never go west after dark.

8

Ivan

Ivan loved the sound of hitchhiker steak frying in a skillet. He loved the sizzle and the aroma, but more than that, he loved it as a reward he gave himself for concocting and carrying out a brilliant ruse that duped not one, but two college girls. He would have meat for maybe a month now. He looked forward to every meal, because with each meal he would relive the entire experience from offering a ride to the final screams in his own meticulously built torture chamber, or "rumpus room" as he liked to call it. Today had been a good day.

He added some seasoning salt and cracked black pepper to the steak, took a deep whiff, and closed his eyes to concentrate on the aroma. When he opened them, he glanced out his kitchen window to catch the last red glow of twilight fading away over the mesa to the west. Ivan loved this country. He loved its isolation and rugged beauty, a wide canyon nestled among high mesas in the high desert with only scattered junipers to provide a sparse cover for game, a single stretch of highway with frequent hitchhikers, and his nearest neighbor over two miles away—much too far to hear even the shrillest, most ear-piercing scream. The devil himself couldn't have designed a better place for Ivan to pursue his sport, he thought.

Ivan glimpsed something move among the silhouettes of juniper to his left. As he watched, he saw four vague outlines swaying in the breeze become four distinct silhouettes walking up his driveway. Guessing they were a family stranded on the highway, Ivan gathered any meat even vaguely human in appearance from the table and hid it in the freezer. He fetched a small pistol from the nearby bedroom and stuck it in his pocket in case he decided not to let them go.

Ivan walked onto the porch when the strangers were a few feet from it. In the light from the kitchen window, he could see a lean, muscular man; a woman that Ivan considered *lean but luscious* and that made his mouth water; a skinny teen-age boy whom Ivan would love to see shiver in horror; and a little girl of about eight who could probably utter a delightful scream of terror at the most innocuous things. They were tanned, well-groomed and wore clean sports clothes. Their faces were open, relaxed, and smiling, though they appeared to be tired. Their image as the stereotypical middle-class family flipped a psychological switch in Ivan sending a bolt of anger blazing through him.

Ivan had no respect for the institution of marriage. He wanted to desecrate it, violate it, just as he wanted to violate the woman...and maybe the little girl...maybe all of them on general principle alone. "Can I help you?" he asked. Ivan used his hatred for all-things-family to create a broad, friendly smile, the first small step in any deception.

"Good evening," said the man. "I'm Henry Carver. This is my wife Emily, my son Bobby, and my daughter Natalie. We were hoping to use your phone to call roadside assistance. Our alternator just died on the highway. We hate to bother you, but we can't get any cell coverage here."

"This area's pretty remote," said Ivan. "A lot of carriers don't reach out here. That's why I don't have a cell phone." An idea emerged in Ivan's mind. "I have a landline, but it's been in and out all day. You're welcome to try it though."

Ivan stepped quickly into the kitchen and pulled out an old inoperable handset from a kitchen junk drawer. Just then Henry opened the kitchen door and the family followed in one after the other. "Here you go," Ivan said handing the handset to Henry. Now, pardon me for a minute. I have to go to the bathroom."

Ivan exited the kitchen, but instead of going to the bathroom, he went to the bedroom, where he disconnected the base for the working handsets from the wall and hid the end of the line behind the nearby dresser.

The meat was sizzling in the pan when Ivan returned to the kitchen. "Mmmm," said the Natalie. "That smells good. What is it?"

"Venison." Ivan wondered if he could stir up some revulsion in Natalie. He would like to see a look of disgust on her sweet, little face. Maybe he could get a tear started. "Y'know...deer...like Bambi."

"Ewww!" said Natalie. Tears started to well up in her big, blue eyes.

"I'm sorry," Ivan said with a grin. "It's not venison. It's pork. I started to put on venison tonight, but I changed my mind at the last minute."

"Pork?" asked Henry. "That doesn't smell quite like pork."

Ivan didn't want to go through the effort of making up lies continuously and he didn't like being contradicted by a perfect little family man like Henry. Torrents of hatred for Henry and for everyone like Henry and Emily flooded Ivan's mind. Ivan wanted to pull his pistol and knee-cap them both then and there, but he didn't. He maintained his cool, disciplined demeanor and lied. "It's a special kind of pork, all the way from Korea. I picked up a taste for it when I was in the army. Would you like some?" Although Ivan was loathe to share any of the pretty hitchhiker's steaks (the first sight of her bare thighs had made Ivan's mouth water even as he had hung her screaming by her heels from his garage rafters), his imagination was intrigued by the range of possible reactions if he were to tell them, after all had had a taste, that tonight's main course had been courtesy of the University of New Mexico.

"No, thanks. We just had a cook-out at Navajo lake. It smells good though. Is there another way we can call out? Maybe e-mail?"

"No, not really." Then he remembered the hitchhiker's cell phone in his bedroom. An unanticipated ring might spoil his ruse. "My brother's cell phone might work. He left it here a few days ago. It's in the bedroom. Let me check it." Ivan had axed his contemptible swine of a brother years ago, but still found it convenient to use him as an excuse occasionally. "Please have a seat while I go look."

The Carvers seated themselves around the kitchen table.

Once in his bedroom, Ivan switched off the hitchhiker's cell phone. He sat on the edge of the bed for a moment devising a plan to establish control over the Carvers quickly without tipping them off that he was up to something. He wanted them to be his. He wanted Emily especially. But if he kept her, he would have to keep them all. On the bright side, he would be able to experiment with children, which he had never done before, and with a grown man, which would be interesting and probably a challenge. Ivan estimated Henry would last probably a lot longer under torture than the others. He might have a lot of fun with Henry. He had always hated that type anyway. Now he had the opportunity to have one at his disposal for as long as he wanted. He might strip away Henry's pretty, smooth, blemish-free skin to see what lay underneath.

Ivan had killed only solitary hitchhikers until yesterday when he scored his first double-header, but here he saw an opportunity that went beyond his most macabre dreams: to have an entire family at his mercy and make them watch each other suffer. Ivan took a deep breath. He noticed his heart had begun beating faster and his breaths were longer and deeper than normal. The thought of having a family watch each member take his or her turn in torment turned him on. He leaned back, closed his eyes, and took a long, slow, deep breath. He felt an erection developing. He opened his eyes and stared ahead. He loved this feeling. He had killed for it many times before.

As lurid images rushed through Ivan's mind of the Carvers squirming under his sadistic control, his pulse quickened, his breathing came more rapidly. A destructive, animalistic sexuality of primal lust and brute force permeated his flesh and bones to his soul's very core. While he had one on the table, the others would be locked in the cell begging for mercy and forgiveness for whatever offenses they had committed against him. He would show them neither. Their very presence offended him. He hated their cleanliness. He hated their wholesomeness. He hated the air they breathed and he would take it from them. He felt people like them had held him beneath contempt for his entire life and now he would turn the tables on as many as he could and he would enjoy every one of their fading heartbeats for as long as he could.

Ivan closed his eyes for a moment to let the delicious thrill surge through his being. He started softly humming a favorite heavy metal tune of sex and violence. The hum grew gradually in intensity. He mouthed the words. He muttered the words. He whispered them. He sang them with a growing power. He thought of opening his fly and masturbating then and there, but he interlaced his fingers behind his head and stretched his back to keep from touching himself. No, he wanted to keep this feeling for as long as possible. He would not touch himself until he had Emily strapped down. Ivan opened his eyes and took a long, deep breath to bring himself back to earth from his diabolic nirvana, so that he could collect his thoughts and pull together a plan.

How to control an entire family? If he just pulled the gun, it would be difficult to watch all four simultaneously until he could herd them into the cage in his basement. Besides, Henry might try to be a hero at his first opportunity and he appeared in good shape. The teenager and Emily were also in good shape and might join the dad in any fracas.

Ivan knew he could physically overpower the mother and each of the kids one on one, but again Henry was the problem. If Ivan gained the upper hand on Henry, the rest would be no problem. Ivan could control them by threatening Henry. Then an idea for a ruse came to him. Ivan pulled his blackjack from the nightstand drawer next to the bed and stuck it in his pocket and headed to the kitchen.

As he walked, Ivan mused over how much he loved trickery. He felt that it was in the practiced art of deception that he proved he was smarter than his prey and that he was a true hunter. Successful hunters were skilled in camouflage. Years of successfully hunting students had taught him how to appear weak and harmless to lure someone into his car or onto his ranch. Then at the critical moment, he would apply one of his many means of immobilizing his prey and his true genius and strength would suddenly appear, often paralyzing the victim with fear or sending them into panic, which Ivan enjoyed more than watching snuff flicks.

Outside the kitchen door, Ivan paused. He could hear Natalie's sweet voice and laughter as she gossiped with her mom about her playmates at school. For a moment, he felt nauseous and weak. He wondered how he had become so evil that he was now about to explore the delights of tormenting children. Still, he would do what he needed to do to subdue his own weakness.

Looking back over the last few years, he could see that although his first kills had plagued him with guilt and paranoia about being caught, he had learned to overcome his revulsion at his own acts and that any guilt would dissipate with time along with the fear of being caught. Mastering guilt and fear strengthened him as a merciless hunter. He had learned self-control as well, which he needed in order to control others. All his experience with the hunt had taught him that he was more disciplined and smarter than anyone else, even than the police with their high-tech crime analysis equipment and forensics. No matter how many he killed, no one could catch him. Now he looked forward to this whole experience of controlling a family, which would teach him how to control a group and how to control his emotions while butchering men, women, and children while they tried to scream through the duct tape sealing their mouths and struggled to break free of Ivan's steel handcuffs. If he could control his emotions while tormenting Natalie, he could control himself while tormenting anyone. If there were a god of evil, the Carvers were his gift of a means to a more powerful existence.

Ivan took a deep breath, hardened his resolve, and entered the kitchen. The Carvers were staring at the sizzling meat, still eyeing it with great curiosity, whispering nervously among themselves.

Ivan cleared his throat. The Carvers turned quickly. Their eyes showed a touch of anxiety that had not been there before. Ivan thought he detected a touch of confusion as well, as if they did not know exactly what to say or do next. They seemed to have lost their self-confidence. Ivan realized that he was sensing incipient fear; its smell was intoxicating.

Ivan addressed Henry. "Sorry, I didn't mean to startle you. Well, my brother's phone is dead, but I'm recharging it now.

It may take a few minutes and I'm not certain even if we're in his carrier's coverage. By the way, could I ask a small favor of you?"

"Okay." Henry's voice seemed to have a slight tremor.

"I have a heavy refrigerator to move in the basement and I haven't had anyone to help me in months. Could you give me a hand? It would just take a minute."

"No, we don't mind. Bobby, let's you and I go help Mr.—?"

"Ramirez."

They started to rise, but Ivan leaned over and whispered in Henry's ear. Time had come for another lie. "You may not want your son to help us. I have some magazine cutouts on the walls that—well, you understand."

"I understand. Bobby, wait here. This will just take a minute."

Ivan led Henry out of the kitchen down a short hall. For a moment Henry worried that the rest of the family might flee, but then he relaxed when he thought that it was a long way to the nearest neighbor and Ivan could simply run them down in his pick-up. They turned left down a flight of steps with a light at the top, but none at the bottom where a closed door could be made out in the dim light. When they reached it, Ivan started fishing in his pocket for his keys."

"I'm just curious, but why didn't your brother help move the refrigerator when he was here?" asked Henry.

"He's in a wheelchair." Ivan took out his keys and started searching for one. He took a couple of steps back up the stairs and behind Henry. "There's better light up here," he said. Ivan searched through the keys until he saw Henry staring at the door with the same perplexed stare he had while watching the hitchhiker fry in the pan.

"That's an interesting smell coming from in there—

Ivan whipped out his blackjack and struck the back of Henry's head. Henry fell against the door and it swung open into a dark room. Ivan jumped over Henry, dragged him inside, closed 1the door, and turned on the light. Inside was what Ivan thought of as his "entertainment center": a homemade rack, irons hanging from the wall, barrels of acid for torture and for disposing of remains, a small cell, a set of bare mattress springs and a generator for what Ivan liked to think of as 'electrotherapy', battery cables, carpentry and automotive tools, and Ivan's pride: a brand new surgical table with lights and surgical instruments.

Ivan dragged Henry to the table, stripped him, and strapped him down. Ivan chuckled imagining the looks of the faces of Henry's family when they saw him strapped down naked and completely at Ivan's mercy. They would do anything to save their dad and Ivan would ask them to step inside the cell. They wouldn't have any choice, because he would lock the exit behind them and he would have the gun. He just had to come up with another excuse to bring them down, but first he would toy with them. Ivan turned out the lights, closed the door, and hurried back to the kitchen.

As soon as he entered, Emily asked, "Where's Henry?"

"He's in the bathroom. I have one in the basement."

"There are no magazines in there, are there?"

"I may have some hunting magazines in there."

"God, he may be in there forever. I thought your pork might burn, so I turned down the heat."

"Good. Thank you." Ivan took a seat at the table. "You're sure you don't want any?" Ivan noticed the throat of Emily's blouse was open and he could run his eyes down her cleavage and see the edge of her brassiere. He imagined running his tongue down her cleavage and licking up blood oozing down from holes in her nipples as she squirmed and tried to scream through the duct tape holding her pouty lips together as Henry's dissected corpse stared at them from the surgical table. Ivan shook himself to wake from his reverie and let out a sigh.

"Is everything okay, Mr. Ramirez?" asked Emily.

"Oh, fine. I get the shivers now and then. My mother used to say it was someone walking on my grave. I'm sorry, did you want some pork?" Ivan smiled imagining Emily's reaction to finding out she had eaten human flesh.

"Maybe later. It might be a while before Henry is finished. I can never get him to eat a balanced meal. He works very hard and doesn't have time for a proper meal."

"What does he do?"

"We own several meat markets in Santa Fe."

Ivan thought the irony was too beautiful to believe. If Henry woke up to find himself marked up with a magic marker like a side of beef into tenderloin, ribs, ham, he would know exactly what was about to happen." Ivan cleared his throat and replied. "Okay, so that's how he knew about the pork in the pan. You say 'we' so it's a family business?"

"It is for Henry and me, but Bobby wants to be a zookeeper as does Natalie."

"Wildlife biologist, mom," said Bobby as if being disparaged.

Ivan ran his eyes up and down Bobby. He imagined him chained naked to the walls trying to scream with his lips sewn shut and eyelids cut off so that he could see everything happening to his mother. Ivan touched himself surreptitiously under the table to make his growing erection more comfortable.

A pack of coyotes started yipping in the distance.

"Disgusting creatures," said Emily.

"You don't like animals?"

"Not all animals. Coyotes are mangy and have ticks."

"But you like dogs, mommy," said Natalie.

"Dogs aren't the same as coyotes, honey," said Emily.

Ivan smiled slightly as he gazed at Natalie, imagining her in the cell, eyes filled with tears, as he walked toward her slowly, scalpel in hand, with pack of caged coyotes feeding on the mutilated corpses of her family in the background. That, he thought, could be a special treat for Natalie.

Emily checked her watch. "Where is Henry? We need to go."

"Follow me," said Ivan. "The kids may want to come along. The entertainment center is in the basement so they can have something to do as they wait."

"Good. I want to have a few words with Henry about making us wait and that may take a while."

Ivan led the way down the hall, but at the top of the stairs he stepped aside and let Emily, Bobby, and Natalie pass down the stairs first. He stuck his hands in his pockets to hide his erection.

Emily opened the door to the dark room. "The lights are out."

"The bulb may have burned out. Go on in. I know where another switch is. The bathroom is in the back."

After the Carvers entered the darkness, Ivan stepped in, drew his pistol, locked the door, and switched on the lights. In the glare of the surgical lights, Ivan saw Emily and Bobby several feet ahead of him blinking as their eyes adjusted to the glare and Natalie stood doing the same a couple of feet to his left. He held the pistol waist high pointed at Emily.

The sight of Henry strapped to the surgical table with gleaming instruments at his side startled Emily and she gasped.

***

Ivan looked up from the spiral notebook on his desk to the other side of the classroom and took a deep breath. He ran the fingers holding his pen across his crewcut, massaged his scalp for a moment, and then pushed his horn-rimmed glasses back up to the bridge of his nose. He set his elbow on his desk and started chewing on the pen's cap end. He breathed deeply, savoring his growing erection. What could he have fictional Ivan do to fictional Emily he wondered. He could have fictional Ivan shackle their imaginary children to the wall then force them and their dad to watch as he raped their mom before their eyes and their dad screamed threats of vengeance as he struggled violently against the straps holding him down. He could have Emily enjoy rough sex. He could bring out a wanton side of her that he like to think the real Emily kept hidden behind the pageboy cut and under the angora sweater. Something that would be too much woman for the real Henry, but not enough for real Ivan.

Somebody lightly smacked the back left of Ivan's head and he snapped around to find out who, but Henry and Emily had already passed him on the right and were snickering as they walked toward the door, their arms tightly around each other's waist. "What's the matter, Ivy? Someone rouse you out of one of some twisted little fantasy? Perv." said Henry.

Emily shoved Henry playfully. "Stop it, Henry. He can't help it if he's a dork." Then she turned grinning to Ivan. "Can you, dorkweed?" She laughed, flashing bone-white teeth hidden behind luscious full red lips. They continued laughing all the way to the door and down the hallway just as the bell rang ending the day.

Ivan hated high school with a passion. He hated senior jocks like Henry Carver in their letter jackets and he hated the princesses like Emily Bates that teased and ridiculed him. There seemed to be no justice in the world. Ivan waited until his erection receded so he wouldn't embarrass himself on his way out, and then he stood, took his leather jacket from the back of his seat, put it on, picked up his books, and headed out to his beat-up 2000 Jeep Cherokee.

Outside, he stopped under an oak next to the parking lot to light a cigarette. He watched Henry and Emily speed down the road in Henry's new bright orange Camaro. "Tonight's Friday," Ivan thought. "Henry will get off work at his dad's store at 9:00, then he will pick up Emily, and they will go parking like they always do on Fridays in the same spot at Navajo lake. I'm tired of all their crap."

Ivan walked to the trunk of his car and opened the lid. Inside was a small duffel bag containing his rape kit: rope, duct tape, a variety of knives and pliers, a wire coat hanger, blindfold, ball gag, assorted sex toys, his .38 revolver with a box of hollow points, and a small skillet with a small camp stove. He made a quick inventory to make sure all was there.

He was doing well, he thought. Though the police had found the body of the first chick, they had not found the most recent two. His skill at concealing bodies was improving. Tonight would be his first try at a double-header and he was looking forward to every second of it. He could feel another erection coming on already.

9

Sorcerer

November 2, 2012

Doc,

I hate to say good-bye like this, especially in light of the debt of gratitude I owe to you for all you have done, but I feel there is nothing left for me in this life but to resurrect my involvement in the black arts, of which I have told you very little.

I am on my way to Chichen Itza, from where I intend to head farther south into Guatemala. Perhaps I shall head on into South America. I have always wanted to see Machu Picchu and the Nazca Plains. Who knows what ancient sources of power I shall find there? I am taking advantage of my new lack of permanent connection to my native land to see the wonders I have wanted to visit for a long time, but for which I never had the time or money, because in my later years I sacrificed those desires for the nobler goal of maintaining a family. Now, with the death of my daughter Christina and her baby Ethan, who never had the chance to open his eyes and see so much as the physician delivering him, that goal has vanished. For the moment, my conscience, or what is left of my conscience, has forced me to sober up and stop long enough at an Internet Café in Chihuahua to send this message.

You are the only psychiatrist I have ever seen, and I cannot thank you enough for the insight you have given me into my own nature and into my perception of the world, when I had to heal from the loss of my only child and grandchild. Of all the hell I have ever experienced, including the death of my wife, my daughter's death during the birth of what would have been my grandson dragged me through more emotional agony than I had ever thought possible. In that moment, I saw her death as the death of my only good legacy to this world. Only now is my mind no longer so clouded with lust for vengeance that I can reflect clearly upon my days as a callous young sorcerer and how much suffering, sorrow, and anguish I caused. Then, with less empathy for others than I have now, I had no hesitation in doling out evil in order to achieve whatever self-serving goals I had at the moment--including seducing as many women as possible. Meeting and getting to know Christina's mother, Agatha, taught me a new perspective on the world, which led to the first and only time I was ever in love, which led to my renunciation of the black arts. Now, even though what I have done to the jerk that seduced Christina can be rationalized as justice, however extreme, I must ask myself about the collateral emotional damage I have inflicted to his family and friends and for which I am responsible.

Admittedly, I bear some responsibility for this entire

tragic scenario, because I was never completely truthful with Christina. From the time she started to show interest in magic, even though it was the harmless white magic that naïve school girls use in a pathetic attempt to get a boyfriend, I warned her against dabbling in magic without revealing my sordid past. For over twenty years, I have tried to forget my past by burying myself in my work as a history professor and a medievalist while rearing my family in the best world I could offer: an idyllic, middle-class neighborhood free of the evil with which the world threatens. But because Christina never knew of my involvement in the black arts, she always treated my warnings with disdain.

I never understood what Christina saw in Brandon. Professing to be a Wiccan, he was different from all the boys she had previously dated. She knew I had an interest in ancient religions from having interrupted my preparations for class occasionally. Maybe she saw a faint similarity between Brandon and myself that spurred her interest in him. Had Brandon actually believed in Wicca, I would have found him only pathetic and not detestable. Based on what Christina told me and from what I had heard from true Wiccans, I could see that he was using Wicca only to seduce any girl he could.

At times, I wish I had met him long before I did. Then maybe I could have scared him off. But as it was, I never met him until after Christina's demise.

As they grew closer, she spent time with him more and more and spoke to me less and less. My heart broke more with each passing day, as I saw the little girl I had raised since her mother's death from cancer drift away from me in spite of my almost daily admonitions. She seemed to forget everything I had ever taught her, taking more and more chances with her young life, ignoring the wisdom I had learned through the school of hard knocks, and holding me in ever greater contempt.

Then one day she came to me to beg forgiveness, the prodigal daughter, after Brandon dumped her when she told him she was pregnant and that she wanted to bear the child she called Ethan (after my father). In my joy of having her back I told her all was forgiven and that I would be there with her every day to raise Ethan until the day I died and even after that, for all I had would go to them.

She wanted Ethan no matter what. I think she saw him as something that gave her life meaning—as I had seen her own birth. Instead of looking at this as some sort of punishment from God for her iniquities, as many young girls would have, she remembered the wonderful childhood she had had with her mother and her maternal, nurturing instincts went into overdrive. She wanted her baby with a passion I had never seen in her before.

Then came the bad news. Her OB/GYN told her that her womb was underdeveloped and that she would probably have problems that would put the lives of both herself and the baby at risk. He recommended an abortion. But, foolishly, Christina put her faith in her Wiccan earth-deities instead of in science, gathered some crystals and herbs around her, said some simple spells and prayers, and pushed on with the birth.

On the day of her death as well as later, on the day of her funeral, Brandon was nowhere to be seen. I found out later from Christina's friends that they had seen him out with a different woman on each day.

I mourned for months, sometimes spontaneously breaking down and sobbing for hours. I did not eat. I slept very little. I drank much. I sought relief from my agony in pills and the latest recreational drugs. I often stared ahead into space with a burning hatred for all things Brandon while trying to focus my mind enough to plot my revenge. Finally, I decided I had to find a way to get my act together for long enough to avenge myself. You never knew this, but that is why I needed your help. I needed someone to help me out of depression long enough so that I could focus my thoughts well enough to plot my vengeance.

I could have used my skills in the black arts to take some form of limited, immediate revenge at any time, but, unlike the movies, the majority of the most powerful spells usually destroy someone some distance away, out of sight, and perhaps several days or weeks later. I wanted to look Brandon in the eyes and see my rage grasp him like talons.

Spells also require a great deal of concentration and self-discipline which I did not have when I first came to you. What I wanted to do to him required even more concentration and more meticulous planning than usual. I wanted to devise a plan in which I could witness his death yet leave no evidence *and* be sufficiently cruel to be entertaining as well as just.

While researching vengeance through my collection of grimoires, the answer became obvious. I did not need a spell of great power. I needed perhaps only a few easy spells and then to seduce him into the realm of black magic in order to lead him to his demise. I loved the delicious irony in seducing the seducer.

I knew from Christina that Brandon liked to hang out in the coffee shop of a local bookstore to talk with his friends, read up on Wiccan practices, and to girl watch (which made her indescribably jealous). My plan was to hang out at the same coffee shop until such time as I could introduce myself. I went through Christina's things and found some photographs of Brandon and a lock of his hair. These were enough of the materials I needed to cast some spells to open him up to meeting me and to becoming involved in the black arts.

When I had given the spells enough time to work, I began to frequent the coffee shop at times I knew he and Christina used to be there. I would take along a book or magazine on magic in order to arouse Brandon's curiosity once I did make contact. I also prepared a simple illusion to impress a novice.

The first few times I saw him he was with friends and this allotted me no opportunity for an introduction. The next time, I was able to take the table next to his. This permitted a chance to politely say hello and for him to eye my books with great curiosity (showing that my spells were working), before one of his friends appeared, which of course was an opportunity to eavesdrop on their conversation while pretending to be engrossed in my book. This enabled me to plan my initial conversation with him. I was also able to learn enough about him to refine my spells of persuasion.

Finally, the opportunity I had awaited arose when I entered the coffee shop and saw the table next to him was unoccupied. He was engrossed in a book about crystals. I snapped up the seat and began reading a book on crystals which I had happened to bring. Before I could initiate the conversation however, he asked the time. A coffee-date he was expecting was late and (he freely admitted) he had left his watch at some other girl's apartment the night before. Just as I answered, the young lady in question walked in appearing to be lost in serious thought. She waved politely to Brandon as she walked over to the counter to purchase a large cup of soda. Then she stepped over to Brandon and threw it in his face (splashing some on me in the process), while calling him a variety of obscene names for which the predominant adjective was "cheating." She then took his watch out of her jeans and threw that at him as well before running sobbing out the door.

To his credit, Brandon retained his cool and apologized to me for his now former girlfriend's behavior. I told him to think nothing of it, and that I had been through the same scenario many times. I motioned to the books he had along and asked if he had an interest in the Wiccan arts.

From there our relationship blossomed over the next few times we met. I continually spurred his interest in the black arts by occasionally hinting at how it could be used to influence actions of others and how one might use it to obtain women. One evening, we talked until the shop closed. On the way to our cars, I sealed his interest by performing my prepared illusion. I snapped my fingers causing my left hand to erupt into flame. After a few seconds, I extinguished it to show him no harm was done. At that point he asked if I would teach him. I agreed with feigned hesitation and swore his secrecy. Then we shook hands and formally introduced ourselves. Of course, I lied and told him my name was John

Dee in case Christina had ever mentioned me. As he started toward his car, he turned and said I seemed familiar to him somehow. I told him that I had heard that remark often, because I looked like a lot of old men.

"That's it!" he said, snapping his fingers in revelation. "I used to date a girl whose dad looked a lot like you. She showed me his picture once."

Then I remembered a photo of myself with Christina that Christina used to carry in her purse. "I wonder if it's the same guy I've heard about," I said. "Did she tell you anything about him?"

"Nothing. Just that she really loved him and admired him, all the usual crap that chicks dish out about their dads. I think he was a professor of something or other. She said he was really intelligent and was always trying to teach her stuff in his way. Do you have any children?"

"No, not now. I used to have one, but...well...things happen. Whatever happened to that girl?"

"I kicked her out when she told me she was knocked up. I told her that she should have used better contraceptives and that it was her mess. I didn't want anything to do with it. I have more chicks and I can't be tied to just one. After all, I have a life to lead." He paused for a moment as if reflecting. I thought I detected a bit of regret in his eyes, but not in his tone. "She died later."

I said I was sorry to hear that.

"Oh, well, it made life easier for me. She was just a chick. Everyone told me I should have gone to the funeral, but, hell, I had a date lined up for that day with a *really* hot chick."

He smiled. "Knocked her up too that day from what I understand. Maybe she'll die too. My luck these days seems pretty good. I seem to be on a roll. You know how it is. Maybe this Wiccan stuff really works." He grinned at me with as evil a grin as I have ever seen.

I forced myself to grin and agree in return as if agreeing with him heart and soul, though it took all my self-control not to throttle him at that point. "Yeah, you bet. I know how it is."

Over the next few months we met in a remote, abandoned farmhouse owned by one of my cousins. During this time, I taught Brandon some basic rituals, which he could have found in any library or on the Internet, if he had had the interest to research the topic in earnest. But my main purpose in arranging these meetings was to elicit from him under assorted pretexts a range of personal objects that I could use in my final spell against him. Among these were another lock of hair, a small phial of his blood, another phial of his sweat, finger- and toenail clippings, and a few more articles of clothing. All of these I either collected from him myself or watched him remove them so that I could be certain they came from him and no one else. I took more photos of him to use in the spells as well. Of the spells I taught him, none could harm me and I could counteract all easily. I took intense pleasure in stringing Brandon along as he had strung along Christina, promising him now and then to teach him the most powerful spells of seduction. Every time I looked at him, I smiled inwardly, visualizing him in the throes of the agony I had selected for him.

When I grew tired of toying with him and I could no

longer stomach the constant tales of his sexual conquests, I told him it was time to graduate to the next level. At our next meeting, we would meet at the farmhouse, but then move on to another location. I would call him with the time and date.

The next day I consulted my grimoires and astrological texts and chose a time when the powers of darkness were at their height. Then I called Brandon to set up the appointment. A week before we were to meet, I went to prepare the site I had chosen and which I had selected when I had first decided upon this course of action: the abandoned St. Ursula Psychiatric Hospital in the remote mountains near Los Alamos.

From my research and from my few fellow sorcerers in the area, I knew it to have been a place of great torment, not only because of the obvious reasons an asylum is feared, but also because during its heyday during the Depression, one of the male attendants had been a serial killer, who had tormented dozens of victims in a basement operating room, before being caught and sentenced to die in the electric chair.

That night I brought my old staff out of storage, gathered some tools and paint, and drove to the site. I cut my way through the chain link fence surrounding the grounds with wire cutters, used a crowbar to break in the main building through a side door, and then made my way by flashlight downstairs to the infamous operating room kicking aside rats and pushing through immense cobwebs along the way. I breathed in the musty smell and dank atmosphere with relish, remembering the many days I had spent in such places as a young sorcerer, casting spells that had successfully doomed my enemies to indescribable torment followed by slow death.

Once I arrived, I pulled out my cell phone and dialed 911 to check the reception (Brandon and I had the same provider). There was none.

I pushed aside the rusted operating tables and antiquated lights to clear the center of the room. I swept the floor with a broom I found nearby and then painted a large double circle containing a pentagram and the names of powerful spirits onto the floor tiles and a smaller circle tangential to it for Brandon, examining the tiles across which Brandon's circle cut in the process. I found a loose one that came up easily from the floor and chipped out a small portion on one edge toward my circle. Then I sharpened the end of the staff to a sharp point using a knife that had been used in a murder (which one of my relatives, and not I, had committed). I practiced standing in my circle and using the sharpened staff point to flip the tile until I could do it easily, refining the staff point and the chipped hole as necessary. I put the tile back in place and left.

For the next several days, I remained in my sorcerer's lair and did nothing but fast, meditate, chant, pray to unholy spirits, and cast spells using most of the items I had collected from Brandon in preparation to conjure the most vile and evil spirits I knew or of which I had read in my grimoires. Except for the light of the 49 red candles lining the walls, I lived in total darkness in a pentagram etched into the wooden floor of my basement. I left it only to use the toilet or to steal pets from neighbors or animals from nearby ranches in order to offer sacrifices to the spirits of the abyss. I abstained from all forms of pleasure and all drugs, herbs, alcohol, or anything that would dull the senses and mind. I drank only enough water to keep me alive. I used the vilest substances I could imagine for incense. I did not bathe, shave, or clean myself in any fashion. I refused to sleep, except for the final day, when I slept in the pentagram without pillow or blanket. I did everything I could imagine to intensify my emotions and magnify my hatred of Brandon.

On the day of our final rendezvous, I cleaned up so that Brandon would not notice anything unusual. I gathered the items we would need for the ritual into a backpack and then I met him at the farmhouse as planned. As soon as we left in my car, Brandon began asking questions, the first of course concerning our destination, which I told him.

"Wow. Spooky. This is real witch stuff. I always thought that these rites were held in spooky places just in the movies, y'know, to make the film spookier for the audience."

"No. Real rites are held in very spooky places. True magic stems from the intensity of the sorcerer's emotions, so the aspects of a rite are designed to stimulate, intensify, and channel the sorcerer's emotions into the direction he desires, whether that be lust, hate, vengeance, or whatever. Paths of magical energy flow throughout the universe. The way the sorcerer influences these is through the energy he generates from within himself in the form of psychic energy and emotions. Meditation stirs the psychic energy and emotions to a degree. The surroundings, scents, alcohol, drugs, herbs, ritual sex, and other things stir the emotions even further."

"Ritual sex?" Brandon's face took on a sudden worried look and he started going for the cell phone in his jeans pocket. "Wait a minute--

"Don't worry. We've never had sex and we're not about to. You've too many Y-chromosomes for my taste."

Brandon let out a sigh of relief and left his cell phone in place. "Okay, then. Good. Nothing against you, but...you understand."

"Yeah, I understand."

"That is a good chick angle though."

"Let's stay focused on the task at hand. Back to my point. Another major factor is the amount of emotions embedded in a place. Like I said, emotions are a form of energy. When intense emotions are aroused, they become embedded in the surroundings. That's why there are ghosts and haunted houses. Ghosts are the spirits and emotions of the tormented and dying that have become one with a location. That's why animals and sometimes people are sacrificed during black rituals. Their emotions during suffering and death soak into the surroundings and into the wizard himself intensifying his power. Where we're going has some of the most intense negative energy in the world embedded in its walls and we're going into its very heart, where we have not only the emotions of a serial killer and his victims, but also those of madmen and patients subjected to primitive psychiatric treatments, such as lobotomies, electro-shock therapy, ice-baths, and who knows what else. I intend to connect with that energy and through it connect with the universal energy paths and use them to best advantage. This place is especially infused with energy because its location is near Los Alamos, where the atomic bomb was developed. The bomb caused an immense amount of suffering in its own right, but all the worries experienced by its creators during its development also generated a lot of negative energy. Also, there are a lot of Anasazi ruins in the area, and so we have all those spirits going back over a thousand years providing energy as well."

"So this place is a little bit of hell."

"Not quite. It's more like a rest stop on the road to hell. You'll see." I tried very hard not to grin or chuckle after making this last statement.

"What are we doing tonight? You've never said."

"I've never said because I didn't want to take the chance you would tell anyone else. I don't think you would, but I couldn't take the chance, even though I think you're ready, because it is a very serious matter. We will be conjuring demons tonight."

"Oh, way cool! This is great. Will we be making them do tricks and stuff?"

I smiled. "Better than that. We're going to bend them to my will."

"How will we do that?"

"Watch and learn." Again, I struggled not to grin.

Although the idea of conjuring demons had excited him initially, from the moment we drove up to the gates I could tell by the nervous shifting of his eyes and the slight trembling of his hands and knees that the surroundings alone were starting to instill fear into his bones. The night was overcast, erasing the stars and moon. The decaying stone walls of the hospital and its entranceway loomed over us as if they were nightmares arising from within a demonic subconscious. A cold front was approaching fast, bringing a stiff, cold northerly wind. As we crawled through the hole I had cut in the chain link fence, Brandon remarked what a terrible night it was. I had to bite my tongue to keep from telling him to enjoy it while he might, because it would be his last. However, to put a fine edge on his emerging terror, I told Brandon the stiff, cold wind reminded me of a stiff, cold corpse. We entered the hospital through the door I had jimmied open. As we stumbled through the litter of yellowing papers, broken glass, and broken chairs in the hallways, our flashlights occasionally caught the yellow eyes of some varmint. I told Brandon they reminded me of the eyes of the damned. I smiled to myself as his trembling increased. More than once, the unexpected scurrying of some wretched rodent startled him and I laughed to myself thinking that he would soon be wishing he were in surroundings as comfortable as these. Somewhere in the stairwell down to the basement, one of the varmints had died and the stench of his rotting carcass permeated the musty air.

"Whew! What died?" asked Brandon, as he started to flail at a large spider web.

"Who cares what *has* died?" I responded curtly. "What's important is what's *going* to die."

Once inside the operating room, I opened the backpack I had prepared and took out forty-nine red candles, incense, our robes, talismans, and several other assorted tools of black magic. I had Brandon place the candles at strategic locations and spray paint several occult symbols on the walls throughout the room according to a diagram I had drawn up. I could have done all this when I had paid my first visit to the hospital, but I wanted the pleasure in watching Brandon unknowingly build his own hellish fate in much the same way as I would have enjoyed watching him dig a grave in which he would be buried alive. After he had finished his allotted tasks and I had prepared the incense, I went into several minutes of intense meditation during which I visualized Brandon burning in the pit of hell.

When I was ready, I had Brandon stand in the center of his circle and I stood in the center of mine. We donned our robes and talismans and I faced north to invoke the northern spirits.

"What do I do?" asked Brandon.

"Much the same as we have done before. Stay right where you are and face me so I can see your eyes. No matter what, do not move outside the circle until I tell you. The circle is your protection against the demons I will be conjuring. They will not cross it. Now, stand quietly."

I held my staff in front of me and I bowed my head, closed my eyes, and fell into a deep meditation for several more minutes on Brandon burning in hellfire. I could hear him shifting his weight from one foot to another as he grew restless. For some reason, I had a vision of him taking his first steps as a child while his parents, watching, laughed with joy, anticipating all the wonderful places his steps would take him. I could only imagine the horror they would experience if they knew those steps had led him here, but I pushed that aside and focused on the task at hand. He had had no mercy on Christina; I would have none on him. I whipped my energy and emotions into intensities that I had never dreamed I could reach. When I opened my eyes to look him in the eye and raised my hands to cast the spell, I felt I had stepped outside human existence and had reached a level of power from which I could command not just demons, but gods as well.

"Hear me, all ye demonic powers of the universe! Asmodeus! Azazel! Belial! Sariel! In the names of all the Lords of Darkness I command ye to appear before me. I command ye to do my will. Appear! Make your presence known!"

The foul aroma of death from the stairwell grew until it was overwhelming. Smells of sulfur and methane arose and the air began to sting my eyes. A low rumbling started in the corners of the room and erupted into the howls of a thousand demons as the air turned stifling hot and a wind from nowhere almost blew out the candles. Then emerged what must have the screams and moans of the damned in the fires of hell and a thousand pairs of demonic eyes appeared, surrounding the circles and focusing on me.

I looked over to Brandon. He was squatting on the floor, covering his head with his hands, and struggling to say the Lord's prayer, which he could not remember and could only stumble over the words: "Our Father, which is in heaven, something be thy name, thy kingdom come...thy kingdom come...on earth something or other-- Oh, God! Help me!" He peered at me from under his hands like a frightened child. He then reached under his robes, pulled out his cell phone, and dialed 911. I knew it was a futile act, but its insolence incensed me, and I knocked it out of his hand with my staff sending it flying towards the door.

"Stand, you coward!" I commanded.

Trembling violently he arose and looked me in the eyes.

I raised my staff above my head and grasp it with both hands and in as loud and as terrifying voice as I could muster,

I shouted: "Brandon Shannon Patrick, for the deaths of my daughter Christina Bryce Thurston and my grandson Ethan Brandon Thurston I hand thee over to all the powers of hell!" All the eyes turned to Brandon. With that, I reached down to the floor with the sharpened tip of my staff and flipped over the tile, breaking Brandon's protective circle. Hundreds of eyes shot into the broken circle and vanished into his body.

The last word I heard Brandon say was when he screamed, "No!" at the top of his lungs just as the demons seized him, throwing him to the floor and twisting his body into strange shapes as boils emerged across his skin. His eyes bulged in terror and excruciating pain. He began speaking in foreign tongues in demonic voices. He vomited, defecated, and urinated upon himself. He cursed all the angels, saints, and heavenly powers. The demons tossed him about the room, slamming him into cabinets, tables, lights, and walls. He screamed the vilest obscenities imaginable. I felt his sweat, tears, and blood splash across my face and I smiled. I watched and laughed as I listened to his joints pop and his bones crack.

For hours I reveled in Brandon's torment, but as dawn approached I knew my powers and thus my defenses against the demons I had conjured would be waning as the sunlight grew, and therefore I decided to end this initial phase of my revenge. I raised my staff again and bid all the demons be gone except for those few hundred that occupied Brandon. The eyes disappeared, the air cooled quickly to its normal level, and the stenches dissipated. As Brandon lay writhing and cursing on the floor, I took my staff and the robes I was wearing, picked up Brandon's cell, gathered the ritual objects back into my backpack, and returned to my car.

There, sitting behind the wheel, I broke down and sobbed until the sun rose over the nearby mountains, not for Brandon, but in release of all the anger and hatred I felt and for the demise of my own soul in returning to that I had renounced. Then I felt a twinge of mercy for Brandon's parents. I did not want them to suffer the agony of not knowing what had happened to their child, a torment I myself would not have been able to bear. I wanted them to be able to find peace at some point in the future. Therefore, I abandoned the second step of my original plan, which was to leave Brandon to the rats. I drove to where I had cell coverage and pulled over to the side to call 911 on Brandon's cell to tell the police where he could be found. I wiped my fingerprints from the cell, smashed it, and threw it down the hillside before driving on to Santa Fe.

From what I have gathered since, a few months after his parents had him committed to a functioning mental institution near Albuquerque, Brandon managed to end his torment in this existence by breaking into the institution's pharmacy and overdosing on painkillers. But his efforts were futile, because the demons would see to it that he entered greater torment on another plane of existence—which had been the aim of my plan all along. If all continues as it should, once I have passed on into that other plane, I will find Brandon and I will add an eternity of torments to his misery as I pursue him throughout all the regions of hell.

There ends that chapter of my life and now I begin another, one composed of dreams I had long ago given up, and which I would willingly give up again, if all could be restored to the way things were.

Farewell, Doc. I wish you a long and happy existence

on this plane and in the hereafter. Should you find yourself among the damned, know that you have a friend in hell.

Sincerely,

Jack Thurston

10

Under the Willow

I was living in Pisté, Mexico, alternating my time between conjuring the spirits of Mayan sorcerers from the nearby ruins of Chichen Itza and losing myself in binges of drunken debauchery with vacationing college girls, when I received a letter from my younger brother in Santa Fe that caused me no small amount of concern.

Unlike me, Bill had always been a simple, good-natured soul. While his beliefs in forgiveness, turning the other cheek, and the inherent goodness of human nature combined endeared him to his family while his I.Q of 80 drew their pity, they also doomed him to fall victim to whatever low-class jerks who happened to wander through his vicinity. What was most tragic about Bill was that deep inside existed a tremendous untapped wellspring of hatred and anger that he could have tapped for his own defense, if for no other reason. However, our parents had instilled in him a great disdain for this unrealized potential, preferring to teach him the way of love and peace, hoping that he could find a good woman one day that would protect and care for him into his old age, but Bill's inherent shyness precluded any such happiness and he remained a bachelor his entire life.

Bill worked as a janitor for the city during the day and bagged groceries on nights and weekends. These long hours enabled him to buy a small, one-bedroom house with a small front yard containing a willow. One of the few pleasures in Bill's life was sitting in a plastic lawn chair underneath that willow on Sunday mornings, watching the traffic pass on the street a few yards away while he drank instant coffee and smoked generic cigarettes and his old mutt Sally laid her head in his lap. On warm nights after work, he and Sally would do the same, but instead of coffee Bill drank cheap beer until he became tipsy and slept until the night air became too cold. Then he and Sally would rise and trundle off to bed, where Sally would sleep on the covers over Bill's feet.

In his letter, Bill asked to borrow a thousand dollars to pay off "debts" he was ashamed to mention. This set off alarms within my mind. Bill never ran up debts. He hated debt. He owned little, but he owed nothing. He felt to owe someone money was to give them power over him and he cherished his personal freedom. Also, he took tremendous personal pride in that he had not asked to borrow money from anyone since he had left had home at seventeen. I sensed something was seriously wrong in his life and I knew I would never be able to find out the truth unless I could look him in the eyes and ask him face to face. I went online and booked an airline reservation from Cancun to Santa Fe to arrive at a time when I knew he would be off work. Once in Santa Fe, I called and asked him to pick me up.

When we met at baggage claim, I spotted him easily because he was wearing a t-shirt with a big smiley face that had the caption underneath: "Keep on smiling!" Bill loved smiley faces and said they helped him keep his spirits up when he was down. He had three on his car, one on the side of his house, and maybe a dozen of various sizes and styles scattered throughout his house. They did not do much for him that day though. I could tell that he had been weeping as he approached.

When close enough, he said only, "I love you, bro" and hugged me tightly. I hugged him, told him that I loved him too, and asked what was up. He picked up my suitcase and we walked in silence to the parking lot, his head bowed in apparent shame the entire way. We were out of the airport and almost to his house before he spoke again and only then after repeated prompting on my part.

"I'll tell you," he said, "but only if you promise not to harm anyone."

"You know I can't do that. I have to keep my word, and I may need the freedom to act as I see fit."

"The last time you acted, someone died."

"I didn't kill him. He killed himself."

"He killed himself in an asylum after you had him possessed by demons."

"True, but let's not digress—"

"I will not let you harm anyone. My conscience won't stand it. If you can't promise not to harm anyone, I'll take you back to the airport now. I can solve my own problems."

"No, you can't. You never could. That's why I came here. You never had the backbone to stand up to people."

"I've always stood up to people."

"Standing there and turning the other cheek while they punch you and steal from you is not standing up for yourself. There's nothing wrong with protecting yourself. I have never understood why you don't. You've always been physically strong. I know there has always been a rage deep inside that you rarely let out, but when you do, it's something to be feared. You can be as vengeful, cold, and ruthless as anyone and probably more than most. Why—?"

"I'm terrified of hurting anyone. That's why. Do you remember the last fight I had?"

"Yeah. In high school. That was cool. You nearly took Woody's head off over that Harrison girl."

"Yeah. Nancy and I had been out a few times. I liked her. She told me that Woody had been hassling her now and then and she wanted me to help her out. I told her I would, but I kept putting it off because, well, I was kind of afraid, considering how big he was and all and I didn't want to fight anyone for that matter. But then one day I snuck into school after cutting class and I found Woody forcing himself on her in that back stairwell next to the chemistry lab. She kept trying to push him away, but he kept trying to kiss her. So I pushed him away and he came at me. I don't remember a lot after that except having him face down on the floor and forcing his left elbow against the joint until it broke. I kept punching him in the sides and listening to his ribs pop. I was going to break his spine, but then the coach and some others pulled me off. The sick thing was that I enjoyed it. I loved listening to the bones snap and to Nancy plead for me not to do anything else. Something evil came out that day. Something I never wanted to face again. I spent some time in reform school for that. The worse thing was that Nancy never wanted anything to do with me again. I think she finally ended up marrying Woody. I saw Woody across a parking lot a few years ago. He still can't straighten out his arm completely.

"I never wanted to experience that again. I didn't want to spend the rest of my life in reform school or prison. So, after that, I put up with a lot of stuff just so evil Bill would never come back. For the most part, I have been happy, but I think you're right. I should have taken my chances. I should have had more guts. There was always that fear of being caught and punished. It held me back, but then it kept me out of trouble too. If I didn't have that, who knows what I would have become? A monster? A murderer? I could've been—

"Me?"

"No, I'm not smart enough to be a wizard or professor or whatever the hell it is you call yourself."

"A sorcerer. Teaching medieval history was my day job, so to speak, just to support my family...the family I used to have."

"Whatever. I'm not smart enough to be any of those. I know you've killed people with that black magic stuff. Is that why you went to Mexico? Were you on the run from the cops or someone?"

"No. Santa Fe just held too many memories for me. After Christina and Ethan died—"

"Ethan? I know your daughter, but who's Ethan?"

"Brandon, the guy I handed over to the demons, knocked up Christina and dumped her. She was going to name the child Ethan, after Dad, but both Christina and Ethan died when she was in the delivery room. I told you all this, haven't I?"

"Most of it."

"Ethan would have been my first and only grandchild." I paused to stifle tears that were forming and to collect myself. "Anyway, I just wanted to go as deep in the jungle as I could and just lose myself in my sorcery and…whatever I could do to take my mind off Christina and Ethan."

"You've killed more people than just Brandon, haven't you?"

"Many more, usually with sorcery, but not always. As I think about it, of the two of us you may be the smarter, because you didn't become me. Your life isn't much, but it's usually peaceful, and you're happy—most of the time. You haven't really done anything to improve the world, but you've never harmed it."

We both paused in a long, uncomfortable silence and stared at the road ahead.

"Look," I said, "I'm your older brother and I love you. I want to help. Please, let me help and I'll promise not to harm anyone and resolve everything peacefully as best I can. Okay?"

"Okay." He paused for a long moment, his face and lips twitching, which I knew were signs that he was doing emotional battle within himself while he tried to find the right words to describe what was happening to him. He took a deep breath and began his story. "A few months ago, a guy named Jimmy Marlboro moved into the trailer park across the street from me. He's a bad dude. He saw me sitting in my chair under my tree one night and came over to bum a cigarette. Then he would come over and bum beer now and then.

It got so annoying that I started to refuse, but he got upset and started saying I was cheap and mean and a lot of other things. I gave in and let him have more beer. Then things just kept getting worse. Soon he was coming around at dinner and bumming a meal, then borrowing tools and not returning them, and then he started asking for money to get his own beer and cigarettes. If I didn't give him money, he would shove me and curse me, telling me I wasn't any good. Then he wanted more and more money. Now, he just comes over and demands money. I wouldn't mind giving it to him, if he was in need, but he has a new motorcycle, he makes a good living in construction, and...uh...one time after I lent him five hundred bucks because he said he needed rent money, I went to the corner store and happened to catch him using it to buy beer and hundreds of lottery tickets. I try to be forgiving, but it's getting to be where I can't support myself."

"Why haven't you called the cops?"

"He's been in enough trouble. I think he's been convicted of two felonies already and if I told on him, they'd send him away for good. I can't do that to anyone."

"You are such a sap." I was so disgusted that I did not speak to him again until we reached his place.

After we stopped in his small driveway, I stepped out and looked over the large weeping willow under which he often sat. It appeared strong and healthy with long pendulous branches heavy with rich green leaves. I looked across the street. Directly opposite sat a house trailer, but catty-cornered to the left a short street led into the trailer park.

"Which is Jimmy's house?" I asked.

"Two houses down the street on the left, the one with the chopper and the pit bull out front."

Though a relatively new mobile home, it seemed to already be in a state of disrepair and neglect with stains and dents visible in the dim street light and a yard cluttered with neglected garden tools and broken lawn furniture. The pit bull paced back and forth at the end of a chain barking and growling without obvious purpose. The motorcycle, a huge Harley, shone in the dim light and was obviously its owner's pride.

"Like something to eat?" asked Bill. "I can heat up some hot dogs and I have some potato salad from the market."

"Sure."

Bill and I headed inside the apartment leaving my bags inside the truck to fetch later. Once inside, Bill started rifling through his fridge looking for the hot dogs while I glanced around his sparsely furnished apartment noting that little had changed since my last visit, except that it seemed unusually quiet. Then I noticed that the food and water dishes for his sweet old mutt Sally were gone. Her leash no longer hung in its usual spot. She did not come out to greet me as she always had before.

"Where's Sally?" I asked.

Bill said nothing. He kept rifling through his fridge.

"Where's Sally, Bill?"

He stood up and faced me. Tears were forming in his eyes. He struggled to answer and finally in a breaking voice, he answered softly. "She's buried underneath the willow."

I looked out the window. I had not noticed before, but at

the foot of the willow in the shadow formed by the nearby streetlight stood a small, white, home-made cross.

"What happened?" I asked. "Don't lie. You're no good at it."

His voice stammered as he told me while fighting back tears. "About two weeks ago, Jimmy came by wanting money. I told him no. He got pissed and left. A couple of days later I went to the grocery and left her hitched in the back yard because it was a beautiful day and I was just going to be gone for a few minutes. When I came back, someone had cut her throat and left her on my front doorstep."

"How much did he want?"

"A thousand."

"I didn't get the letter until—"

"He couldn't wait."

"Why didn't you do something? You could at least have called the cops!"

"I wanted to kill him. I was the angriest I have ever been. I started to go after him, but I stopped before I crossed the street. I wanted to tear him apart, but I'm afraid. I'm afraid of what I'll become. I'm afraid that I'll go to prison and lose my home and everything and I'll have to spend the rest of my life angry and hating and fighting for my life until somebody finally kills me. I don't want to live like that. I dropped to my knees and started screaming. I saw him looking out his window at me and laughing. So finally I called the cops. They came and talked to me and then to him, and then they searched his place, but they found nothing and they left. All they did was to tell me to stay away from him and call a lawyer. Since then, he hasn't come by, but every time he sees me he scowls at me, gives me the finger, and then laughs. He laughs at me and I can't bring myself to do anything."

Bill broke down sobbing and sat on the kitchen floor. I sat down next to him and put my arm around his shoulders. He sobbed for over half an hour. I said nothing, knowing there was nothing I could say that would comfort him, so I just sat with him, holding him tightly, the rage welling within me.

When he had collected himself, he found the hot dogs and boiled them without saying a word while I stood by quietly. We both knew what the other was thinking and we both knew we would not change the other's mind.

When the hot dogs were finished, we took the potato salad from the fridge along with the two last beers and a kitchen chair for myself, and went out to his chair underneath the willow. Beside his chair sat a small, plastic table where we placed the food, but neither of us ate. We opened the beers, toasted to better times, and stared at Sally's grave in silence while sipping our brews.

After a few minutes, I broke the awful silence. "I think Sally will still be with you whenever you sit under this tree. I know a lot of people don't believe animals have souls, but I can't see a good old girl like Sally not having one."

"Sally definitely had a soul," said Bill. "A very gentle, kind, loving soul. I miss her very much. I wanted to get her cremated so that she could be buried with me when I go, but I don't have the money since Jimmy's been around. And I doubt the city will let me be buried here, so I don't know what I'll do."

I started to say something about Bill now having to lie in

the bed he had made, but he hurt enough already, so I held my tongue.

Bill continued. "I always wanted to be buried here anyway. I love this old tree. It gives good shade from the sun in the day and from the streetlights at night. The air always seems to be fresh under it and the leaves rustling almost sound like someone whispering. I got this house the same year I got Sally, so I've known Sally and this tree almost the same length of time. I think they've been my best friends that whole time."

I tossed back the last of my beer as Bill tossed back the last of his. "Let me have your car keys. I'll go get some more," I said.

"I'll go," said Bill.

"No, just write this off as me helping pay my way. It's like my hotel bill, which would be a lot more if I didn't have you to stay with."

"Alright. I'm too tired to argue and you would argue with me about this until dawn anyway. Go down the street to the first stoplight and take a left. There's a Safeway about a mile down on the right." He tossed me the keys and I left.

At Safeway, I was the last customer for the day and they locked the doors behind me just as I entered. I picked up half a case of good Mexican beer, which I estimated would last us the rest of the night.

The checkout girl was cute and mentioned something about never having tried Mexican beer. Though I wanted to get back to Bill soon, I also did not want to pass on an opportunity for a little self-indulgence, which I thought I deserved considering how much of my own time and money I had spent on this uncharacteristically selfless effort to help out my brother. I felt Bill would understand if I told him that I took some time to chat up a chick and make a date for later in the week. We talked for a few minutes and she clocked out a little early so we could sit on the tailgate of Bill's truck and have a couple of beers and share a joint she happened to have. We made a date to go dancing on Saturday night on which I would bring Bill and some tequila and she would bring her wallflower cousin and some grass.

When I arrived at Bill's, the yard was empty and the front door was open. I saw no movement inside, so I thought Bill might have fallen asleep on the couch waiting for me. Instead, as soon as I stepped into the living room, I saw Bill lying on the carpet with a switchblade sticking from his heart. He had been stabbed several times, his shirt torn open, and into his chest had been carved a smiley face the size of a dinner plate. Blood was everywhere. The house had been ransacked. I knelt on the floor beside Bill and wept and wailed and pounded my fists against the bloody floor in frustration for a long time.

When I regained my composure, I closed the door so no one could see from the street and I began planning a pure and personal vengeance that only I could deliver.

I prepared Bill for burial by washing him in the bathtub and putting on him the best clean jeans I could find in his dresser, his sandals, and his favorite Beach Boys t-shirt and laid him out in his bed, between the sheets. I took his favorite possessions: his pocket-knife, his favorite coffee-mug, and the only book he had (a copy of Kipling's *Just So Stories* that he had read over and over), and put them aside to be buried with him later. Then I went to an all-night convenience store and bought a carton of his favorite cigarettes, a six-pack of his favorite beer, and a jar of his favorite instant coffee and set those aside to be buried with him as well. I did not sleep that night. Instead, I knelt beside the bed, stared at his wounds, and focused the anger within me.

The next day I searched Santa Fe for *yerberías*, where I could buy herbs and other items of use to a shaman, and for shops where I could buy occult supplies for pagan rituals and sorcery. I also went to a tattoo parlor and had Bill's full name inked across my heart so that when needed, I could focus on it during the ceremony to come.

When I had the items I needed, I returned to Bill's place, drew the blinds, moved the living room furniture, drew a large pentagram on the floor, and moved Bill to its center. I removed all pictures and decorations from the walls and in their place drew the hundreds of occult symbols I would need and also on the ceiling and floor. I set out the red candles, incense, and other items for the sorcery I was to cast. I changed into the bloody clothes Bill was wearing when he was murdered and knelt beside him. I used the murder weapon to carve a smiley face into my own flesh as it had been carved into Bill, not so deep as to cause serious harm, but deep enough to cause substantial pain on which I could focus. I began to chant and meditate calling upon all the powers of heaven, hell, and those of dimensions beyond to grant me the powers I would need and to enable me to focus the energies of the universe to my will. During the first day, that was all I did. I ate or drank nothing. I did not wash or clean myself in any way. I refrained from defecating or urinating.

The first spell I cast was one of invisibility, so that when anyone passing by looked at the yard it would appear as it had on the day before Bill's death. When the casting was finished, I waited until midnight and then I dug Bill's grave next to Sally's and in it placed him along with his possessions and the gifts I had chosen for his journey into the next world. After the last shovelful of earth was over Bill, I knelt beside him and meditated a while longer. I left the spell in place so that I could monitor Jimmy later without being seen. At that point, I had to sleep because I was losing my ability to concentrate. I slipped into Bill's bed, between the same sheets where I had laid him out, and focused on their feel and the feel of the dried blood in his clothes, which I still wore, until I fell asleep.

The next morning, I woke about seven as the sun came in through the bedroom windows. I rose, and, taking a cheap pair of binoculars I noticed on a shelf, sat in Bill's lawn chair under the willow, so that I could get a good look at Jimmy and burn his face into my mind. I hoped he had not already left for work and he hadn't. In a few minutes he came out of his place and mounted his motorcycle. He didn't wear a helmet, so I had a good look as he stopped at the intersection for a passing pick-up and then rode past Bill's place, staring at the front door, probably wondering if anyone had found Bill's body.

Jimmy was a man of slightly less than average height, but he was wiry and his physique was well-defined. He had a long, bright red Mohawk that reminded me of flames as it trailed in the breeze. I could not see his eyes because of his wraparound shades, but judging by the crow's feet, the creases in his face, his physique, and his scowl I placed him at around forty. He wore a large pentagram on a chain about his neck and wore the colors of a gang called "Hell's Heroes". I chuckled to myself trying to imagine him trying to be a hero while being twisted and tormented by demons among the sparks and acrid fumes of damnation.

I went back into the house, drew the blinds, lit my candles and incense, knelt in the pentagram and circle I had drawn, and started planning my next spell. I tried to concentrate on visualizing the torments I wanted him to suffer, but this was difficult, because I had so many emotions, images, and options rampaging through my mind. I felt overwhelmed by a psychological tsunami. I meditated for a long time until I could focus individually on each of the images flooding my psyche. I thought of the most horrific retributions I had inflicted or of which I had heard throughout the history of sorcery. I decided upon the one that I had inflicted upon the young man I held responsible for the death of my daughter and her unborn child: demon possession. Underneath the willow, I would create a special circle that would contain demons while not allowing them to escape, in effect, a demon cage. I could create the circle and summon the demons easily enough with a day or two of rituals and preparations. The trick would be luring Jimmy into the circle, but once he was there, I could sit back in Bill's chair, have a few beers, and watch Jimmy go through the tortures of the damned while within sight of his own home and the spell of invisibility protected us from prying eyes. It would be like a horror movie on three-dimensional television that I could keep going for hours.

The only glitch might be if someone walking along the street for whatever reason decided to walk under the willow. The spell of invisibility acts as a nebulous dome. All outside the dome see what the wizard wants them to see, but they can walk through the dome easily. Once inside the dome, their vision becomes clearer and clearer the closer they come to the center. Of course, in this instance, the demonic cell would be in the center. Anyone entering it would suffer a rather extreme punishment for trespassing, but then they shouldn't be trespassing.

The next day, under the cover of the spell of invisibility, I laid out the circle, actually three concentric circles enclosing two rings of ancient symbols, three inches below the dirt under the willow so that a shambling footstep by Jimmy would not break it. The rings and symbols were of materials I knew demons would not cross. The center, the actual cage, was empty and large to make it relatively easy to lure Jimmy into the danger zone.

For the following two days I fasted and stayed within my own circle in the living room still in my brother's clothes casting a spell to summon as many demons as I could into the cage beneath the willow instantly upon my signal, which would be to plunge the switchblade with which Bill had been killed into the ground.

The day I was to have my vengeance, I sat in Bill's chair under the willow alternately meditating, reciting chants, and watching Jimmy's comings and goings. Whenever he passed Bill's house, he would look at it intensely as if expecting to see something, which I suspected would be the police. He had to know something was wrong because of the lack of activity. In the back of his mind, he had to be going over what evidence he had left behind and wondering when the police would find it. Still he had to have sufficient confidence that he had left nothing incriminating or he would probably have fled the state. Whatever the case, he had to have guts to still live within sight of where he had committed a murder and to believe that he would not become a suspect.

Then I knew how I could lure him into the circle. I would lift the spell of invisibility for him and no one else. At night I would sit in Bill's chair in his clothes, smoking and drinking beer as Bill had. Bill and I looked sufficiently alike that at night Jimmy could easily mistake me for Bill. Once Jimmy saw Bill and believed he was still alive, he would have to come over to silence him. Given what I perceived to be the hot-headed nature of his temperament, I believed that if Jimmy saw Bill sitting under the willow, Jimmy would be over in a flash.

Now the only thing I lacked for my sorcery to be successful was a personal item of Jimmy's that only he and no one else owned or used, within the circle. This would enable the demons to target the right person. The only object I knew that I could positively identify as belonging to Jimmy and to no one else, would be a snippet of that flaming red Mohawk and to be absolutely certain I would have to cut it from him myself. I would also need it to lift the spell of invisibility for him personally.

The obvious solution was to slip into his mobile home one night as he lay asleep and cut it from his head. Unfortunately,

I could not cast a spell of deep sleep upon him, because, iron-ically, I would have to have one of his personal items (though I had the switchblade, I could not be certain that it was not borrowed or stolen from someone else). I could also not cast a spell of confusion around myself personally, because casting a spell to move with a person is more complex and requires much time. I wanted to have my vengeance as soon a possi-ble. I would have to take my chances as would any common burglar, but I have always been an excellent thief, so I fore-saw no problem with sneaking in and out of Jimmy's place. I planned to break in that night at 3:00 a.m. when my powers were at their height based on astrology.

A little after 2:00 I dressed in a black t-shirt and dark blue jeans with black sneakers and thin nylon medical gloves, but did not smear shoe polish on my face or anything else like a burglar in the movies. I placed the switchblade in my right front pocket in case things went awry and I had to fight for my life. The only gun Bill had was a .22 rifle he kept for killing varmints—a rather awkward weapon for car-rying during a break-in. In my left front pocket, I placed a small pair of scissors and a plastic bag to contain the clip-ping. In my right rear pocket, I placed a small screwdriver and some other small tools to pick a door lock or open a win-dow. I mixed some raw hamburger with the powder of about a dozen crushed sleeping pills, formed it into a patty and put it in another plastic bag, which I carried in my right hand.

At 2:55 I walked to the street and scoped out the area to make sure no one was around. I walked toward Jimmy's trailer. When his pit bull started barking, I took out the ham-burger and threw it to him. He wolfed it down and in a few minutes I was stepping over him to peer into Jimmy's windows to make sure he was not up while also checking to see if any were open. Fortune was with me and I found one near his front door that was open just enough that I could insert my hands to unfasten the latches and raise it.

I crept through the trailer checking each room to make sure Jimmy and I were the only two present. At last I came to his bedroom and peeped through the door. The head of the bed was against the opposite wall. In the light of the full moon I could see Jimmy lying on his right side with his right hand under his pillow and his back toward me. He was snoring. I focused my attention on his eyes to make sure they did not move or turn in my direction. In doing so, as I took my first step into the bedroom, I stubbed my toe against a low, heavy wooden chair sitting next to the door. It squeaked slightly against the floor. I froze. Jimmy did not move. He continued snoring. I crept to the side of the bed behind Jimmy's back, slowly removed the scissors and bag, leaned far across the bed without touching it (though for one heartbeat I almost lost my balance and fell onto it), quickly cut a thumb-sized piece from the end of his Mohawk, and put it into the bag and the bag and scissors back into my pocket.

When I was almost to the door, I turned to watch him sleep. I smiled, gloating that this would be the last night he would ever see rest in the comfort and security of his own home as well as the last night he would ever draw breath again. "Dream," I whispered. "Dream on. Hell knows no rest, only a single, endless night of torment for an infinite morass of the damned. Though, if I could, I would have you spend these last few hours before dawn in night terrors, screaming at visions of what lies waiting for you."

As I turned to exit and took a step, my toe hit an empty beer bottle beside the chair and sent it clattering across the floor and against the wall. I glanced back just as Jimmy whipped a pistol from under his pillow, yelled "Bastard!", and fired, hitting me in the left bicep as I turned to run.

I bolted through the trailer, Jimmy only a few steps behind in nothing but his shorts. I sprinted across Jimmy's yard, leapt over his sleeping watch dog, and bolted across the street, thinking that maybe I could reach the .22. I ran under the willow hoping the spell of confusion would hide me, but he was too close. He fired again and hit my left thigh, probably trying to stop me rather than kill me. I tumbled just as I was about to exit the circle and crashed against Bill's chair and table, knocking them over. I rolled onto my back and saw I was just outside the circle as Jimmy stopped in its center taking aim at my face. I thrust my hand into my jeans pocket and pulled the switchblade to jam it into the ground, but Jimmy fired, hitting my right forearm once. I dropped the switchblade. He pointed the pistol at my face. It was a .38 snub nose.

Jimmy had a puzzled expression. "You're not Bill," he said. "Who are you?"

"I'm the man that'll be waiting for you in hell," I said.

"Whatever," said Jimmy. He cocked the hammer.

Then the leaves and branches of the willow rustled and I thought I heard Bill whisper "No!" from somewhere above.

Jimmy and I glanced up just as the willow's branches suddenly reached down, wrapped around Jimmy's body and limbs, and lifted him ten feet off the ground. He started to scream, but a branch entwined itself around his throat and began to strangle him. I could see the branches of the willow pulling and pushing in a hundred directions and heard the sounds of a bone cracking. Jimmy tried to scream, but all he could produce was a harsh gurgling as the branch maintained a tight grip around his throat.

The willow did not dispatch Jimmy quickly. First, it broke an arm. Several seconds later, a leg snapped with a loud pop. Half a minute after that, the other arm broke. All the while the branches tightened around his chest so that even if he was not being strangled, he would find it increasingly difficult to draw breath. Tears flowed. He tried to scream many times, but could not. The willow doubled him slowly backwards to break his spine.

Just then, a police cruiser with its lights on pulled up in front of the willow while another pulled up in front of Jimmy's trailer. Four officers exited the cruisers, all with their hands on their weapons, and began looking at Jimmy's trailer and scanning the neighborhood. The two at Jimmy's place saw the pit bull lying in the yard and the door Jimmy had left open. They drew their weapons and shouted "Police! Sir, are you all right?" into the trailer. Receiving no answer, they entered, still shouting their identity. An officer from the cruiser near the willow ran across the street and waited at the trailer's front door, weapon drawn, for his colleagues to return.

The officer remaining at the cruiser next to the willow was a young, sandy-haired man that I assumed to be new to the Force by the nervous, bewildered look on his face. He kept glancing about in all directions as if the slightest sound were a threat.

Another bone popped and the young officer whipped his face around up toward Jimmy. He pointed his weapon toward the top of the willow. Though the spell of confusion could mask objects from the eyes, it did nothing for masking sounds. The officer's eyes searched the tree top and wherever his eyes looked he pointed his weapon. He moved slowly, cautiously around the tree in a wide circle that kept him just outside the spell's dome. Jimmy let out a loud gurgle, and the officer stepped forward to the edge of the dome. Still, he could see nothing in the tree or in the yard, but he kept hearing sounds for which he could see no explanation. Jimmy moaned and the officer took another step forward and broke the edge of the dome. Once inside, he squinted as if he were trying to see through a cloud. He looked straight at me and rubbed his eyes with his left hand as if he were trying to clear something blurring his vision. Jimmy moaned again and the officer jerked his face up, squinted, and then rubbed his eyes again. I could tell he could make out something, but could not tell what it was.

A call came over his radio and he answered. His colleagues had found nothing in the trailer. They wanted to talk about how to proceed. The young officer holstered his weapon and said he would be right over. He turned and hurried across the street.

While Jimmy continued to gurgle and moan, the officers in his yard talked. A woman from a neighboring trailer stepped out of her door, said something to the officers, and pointed in the direction of the willow. Two of the officers got into the cruiser next to the trailer and drove off to the left in a hurry to circle around to the back. The two that came in the cruiser next to the willow came across to Bill's house, walked up his drive on the other side of his truck so that they did not come under the willow, and knocked on his door. The sandy-haired officer stayed close to the house and circled around to the back yard, while his colleague continued to knock on the door, identifying himself as the police, and waited for an answer that never came. In a few minutes, the sandy-haired officer returned and told his partner that he had found nothing. As they returned to their cruiser the sandy-haired officer kept looking into the top of the willow as if searching for something.

Once the police had left, the willow continued breaking Jimmy's bones snapping one every few seconds. After several minutes, the willow bent him backwards until his spine snapped and then it dropped him. Jimmy hit the ground with a soft thud and lay there staring at me with his limbs in unnatural positions. He was not breathing.

I looked up into the willow and said, "Bill?"

The wind picked up and the leaves rustled. As they rustled, I could make out Bill's voice whispering, "I love you, bro'. I love you, bro'. I love you, bro'."

"I love you, too," I said. "Thank you."

I rose and, hopping on my good leg, hobbled into the house, where I bandaged my wounds to keep me alive until the next day, when I could look up a doctor I knew from my old days in Santa Fe, who would fix me up with no questions asked. Soon after I closed the front door behind me, more police began arriving and searching the area. I kept the lights off and stayed low so that even if they looked in through the windows they could not see me. Again, fortune was with me and none happened to cross under the willow that night. The next night, again about 3:00 a.m., I took Jimmy back to his trailer, laid him in his bed, and placed an anonymous call from his phone to 911 that Jimmy was back and dead and the door would be left open. I went back to Bill's place and watched until the cops came, investigated, and departed with Jimmy's body several hours later.

The following day, I called the police to tell them I was Bill's brother and that I had just shown up for a visit only to find Bill missing. That started the process by which he could be declared legally dead and his last wishes fulfilled in accordance with his will. I stayed at Bill's house until all the legal proceedings were finished, and though I sat under that willow many times before I left, often talking with it as I had with Bill, it never acted or spoke again. When the house was finally sold, the day before the new owners (who loved the willow, by the way) moved in, I destroyed the circles under the soil, packed up, said good-bye to Bill and Sally, gave the willow a final hug, and took a waiting cab for the airport.

I cannot say with any certainty, but now at night, when I sit in my own yard outside Pisté having a smoke and a beer, when the wind blows, I think I hear Bill's voice in the rustling palms saying, "I love you, bro', I love you, bro', I love you, bro'"

11

Alien Embrace

Logan was trapped in a lucid nightmare: in a blurry, twilight world of indistinguishable gray shapes scurrying about clicking furiously, a faceless silhouette was boring a hole into the back of his head. Logan tried to scream, but his mouth would not open. He tried to move, but he felt bound by not only something around his chest and arms, but also by a powerful narcotic that made him feel as if the slightest motion struggled against tons of warm mud pressing against every square inch of his body. Then the drilling seemed to break through the final millimeter of Logan's cranium and the pain disappeared, replaced with a numbing blackness.

When Logan opened his eyes, he was at home in Danville, with his wife Hannah sleeping on his shoulder, her long hair brushing lightly against his face in a tickling, golden wave. He rolled his head slowly toward the window to watch the sun rise over the lush pasture of the horse farm to the east. Soon, he would have to rise and drive downtown to open the hardware store, but for now he would lie under the down-filled comforter and enjoy Hannah's warmth as her breath stirred the hair on his bare chest until the alarm rang or the kids woke, whichever came first. Still feeling drowsy, though still a bit tense from the nightmare, Logan closed his eyes for a moment and took a slow, deep breath, to relax and center himself before rising, but instead drifted back into his nightmare.

In his hazy, gray hell Logan's first and most distinct perception was that although he could feel his arms and legs, he could move them very little. He seemed confined by three segmented steel bands across his torso. He could not move his head in any direction. His vision was still blurry, and he could still hear clicking, but now he noticed that the atmosphere was hot, humid, and musty. The bands were restricting his breathing slightly, but as he took a deep breath, they seemed to expand just enough so that he could breathe a bit more easily, but still keep him confined. He felt something like gas pains encircling his stomach. He gritted his teeth, let out a low moan, and passed into unconsciousness, waking up once again with Hannah. Afraid of falling asleep again and regressing into his nightmare, Logan rose quickly from his bed, leaving Hannah's warmth and the delicate aroma of her perfume behind, and stumbled to the bathroom to begin his morning routine.

#

In a humid cave a few meters below the thick, equatorial vegetation on the planet Stheno D, a creature known to its kindred as Kekla stood in its underground lair on its two hindmost legs, embracing Lieutenant Logan Rickover, the new-found host for its brood, from behind, its flexible ovipositor curving around and inserted into his abdomen above the navel, as Kekla slowly deposited four fist-sized eggs.

Kekla's species was the most advanced on Stheno D. Closest to what inhabitants of Earth would consider gigantic beetles, Kekla's brain and intelligence equated most closely to that of a Neanderthal. For the moment, all Kekla's thoughts and emotions were focused on Logan.

Kekla loved the feel of Logan's body. As it wrapped four of its six armored legs around Logan to immobilize him, Kekla found it soft and yielding, a bizarre experience for a creature whose exterior consisted mostly of segmented, armored shells overlaying a small, soft abdomen. Even more bizarre was the feeling of Logan taking in oxygen through his face and into his chest, unlike Kekla's species, which absorbed the atmosphere through holes in its abdomen and legs.

Though Logan was far different from Kekla's own race, Kekla loved him with all its being, not only because his warm, soft body made it a superb host for Kekla's brood, but also because wrapping its legs around that same warm, soft body gave Kekla a scintillating pleasure that it had never experienced. Logan moved and Kekla tightened its grip, reveling in the new, hedonistic sensation. The thought that such exotic, useful, sensuous creatures exist fascinated Kekla.

Kekla noticed that Logan's breathing was growing quicker and shallower. Kekla was reluctant to let go of him and lose the new-found eroticism that he had brought into Kekla's life, but neither did it want to see Logan die before his time.

Kekla loosened its grip slowly until Logan was breathing freely again, but not so much that he could wriggle free.

Kekla could not afford to let Logan escape. This would be Kekla's only brood for the year. After being deposited, Kekla's eggs needed a week to hatch and then to spend at least a few hours feeding on their host while its meat was fresh and its blood rich in oxygen in order to ensure their survival during this phase of their lives. Furthermore, the pleasure Kekla experienced in seeing its offspring, drenched in blood and sated from feasting, emerge from the carcass of their host far outweighed any passing sensation of erotic pleasure that any creature, native or alien, could instill. Until they became adults in two Stheno years, the primary focus of Kekla's existence would be the survival of the young.

In contrast to all the mental and emotional pleasures Kekla received from watching its young throughout their growth, there was one moment that Kekla hated with a passion: watching its hosts die. Unfortunately, that was one of the most fundamental and cruelest characteristics of reproduction for Kekla's species: to bring new life into the world, an old life, the host, had to be sacrificed.

Love, as humans know it, did not exist on Stheno D. The closest feeling in Kekla's race could perhaps be described best as an instinctive, impassioned fascination that breeders experienced with the creatures that seemed to be the best host for their eggs. The fascination formed rapidly when the brooder spotted a potential host and persisted as its eggs were generated asexually, deposited into their host's body, incubated, and to the moment the newly hatched offspring chewed their way out of the still living host's body. The fascination also instilled a nurturing instinct in the brooder that ensured a host received the necessary nutrients during incubation to keep it alive and placid during the week-long hatching via a tube from the breeder's abdomen inserted directly into the host's stomach. Through a needle-like tube inserted a short distance into the brain, the host received painkillers and hallucinogens that not only instilled intense sensations of pleasure, peace, and euphoria, but also distorted the host's perception of time to keep the host relaxed and quiet while clasped against the breeder's soft underside. About the time the eggs started to hatch, the breeder's supply of nutrients, painkillers, and hallucinogens would run out and the host would waken and start thrashing violently once it saw its surroundings and the pain started to intensify. To avoid injury, the breeder would withdraw the ovipositor and tube and allow the host to drop to the floor to scream and thrash about, dying slowly in excruciating pain as the young fed on its organs and flesh.

By means of the tube inserted into Logan's brain, Kekla could read his mind. Kekla recognized that a human's mating system was radically different from its own and pitied Logan for the torments he would have to endure to bear its, a stranger's, offspring. Kekla received no pleasure from seeing any being suffer. Still, the only thing truly important for Kekla was that its brood have fresh meat for the first hours of their lives.

Kekla recalled fondly the overwhelming desire that arose, when it first spied Logan walking alone among the giant ferns and primitive conifers near Kekla's lair, making his way back to his companions and their spacecraft. Kekla followed him for a short distance, circling, watching from behind bushes, marveling at his two-legged walk and at the suppleness of his body, before bolting ahead and lying in wait for the perfect opportunity to drag him back to the lair.

Now as they stood bound in an alien embrace, Kekla feeding Logan nutrients and hallucinations, Kekla worried if the damage done by the tubes inserted into Logan would kill him before the young hatched. Kekla cleared its mind and concentrated on Logan's brain, so that it could experience the same sensations as Logan to ensure that they were pleasurable. As Kekla concentrated, the surroundings of its lair were replaced with distorted visions of Logan's home which clarified quickly as their minds become one.

#

"Is this really my life?" thought Logan as he lay on his right side, trying to fall asleep as his wife, Hannah, embraced him from behind. He sighed as he listened to Hannah's gentle breath. Hannah has been holding him very tightly for a while tonight, but just now she loosened her embrace and he could breathe again.

"What has happened to my life? How did I come to be here?" Logan thought as he reviewed his life in his mind. "Sometimes I feel like I have always been here with Hannah. There was nothing before her and there will be nothing after her. I cannot remember how we met and I have only vague memories of my childhood. If I did not have her, my life would be so empty and drab. Owning a hardware store in a small Kentucky town is as boring as life can get, but it is peaceful, and I love my wife and my sons, whom I love watching grow and become men. For me, this feels like paradise, but time has passed so fast and everything outside my life with Hannah is mostly a blur with only a few clear memories to call my own.

"I do remember that I had big dreams when I was young and that I wanted to be an astronaut. I still dream about visiting other worlds. Sometimes the dreams are so vivid I could swear they are memories and not dreams. I think they're called lucid dreams. They're always about being an astronaut and usually about being in a jungle on another planet. If I concentrate, I can almost feel the humid, alien atmosphere, smell the strange flowers, and hear the rustling of creatures in the nearby bush. Then the dream turns into a nightmare as something lunges from the undergrowth and drags me along the ground. I scream for help, but no one comes. I can't raise my head high enough to see it, but its claws around my ankles feel like shackles.

Then I awake and find myself in Hannah's arms, my head on my own pillow, the March wind whistling around the corner of our house, and I feel safe and secure and exquisitely happy."

"I had that dream again," he said to Hannah, even though he knew her to be asleep. "Something must be wrong with me. I have that dream so often. I even have flashes of it when I'm awake. I also have flashes about what life must be like as an astronaut. I see myself doing my first anti-gravity training. I see myself stepping onto the moon's surface for the first time and feeling that I have finally achieved my boyhood dream and the whole of the Milky Way is now mine for the asking. I see myself breaking the light barrier for the first time on board a spaceship as we head for Alpha Centauri on my first deployment, to Sirius on my second, Pollux on my third, and then to one more, but I can't recall its name. All these seem so real. How could they just have been my imagination? How could I imagine things in such detail? I must have lived them in another life. If I concentrate, I can picture details as clearly as if they were memories."

#

Kekla sensed a loss of control over Logan's thoughts. Flashes of his actual life were seeping through the haze of hallucinogens. Kekla had seen this before, though rarely, when the host had a body chemistry Kekla had not previously experienced, and the host had an exceptionally perceptive, analytical mind. Both factors seemed to be at work in this instance. Kekla concentrated and increased the dosage of hallucinogens.

#

In his mind, Logan drifted off to sleep in Hannah's arms, feeling the silkiness of her long, blonde hair across his face, sensing the warmth of her body against his, and savoring the aroma of the green apple-scented shampoo she always used. The clock on the nightstand read 2:00 when he passed drowsily into sleep, but it read 2:22 when he woke again with the nagging question of how he and Hannah met foremost in his mind. In the short while he had been asleep, he had dreamed of seeing her first on board a starship. She was a lieutenant in the ship's administration division and she had an incredibly erotic *je ne sais quois* about her. Logan had struck up the first conversation with her in an elevator by commenting on the light reflecting in her opal earrings.

But that was a dream. He had spent his entire life in Danville, except for those four years when he attended the university in Richmond. He must have met her there, but he couldn't recall how.

While he searched his memories by trying to visualize the students in his undergraduate classes, he drifted off to sleep to experience a lucid dream of having his first bridge watch on the starship Venture. He saw himself taking his station with trepidation that he still felt running through his body and down his spine and the wonderful relief and pride when he passed the watch to the next officer who relieved him. The dream was so detailed, Logan could see the sclera in his relief's eyes as they saluted each other, but then the relief's eyes morphed into the soulless eyes of a spider and Logan bolted upright in bed in a cold sweat with his heart pounding. Logan looked to Hannah and saw her sleeping peacefully. He lay down with his back against her front. He picked up her left arm and draped it over him as if it were a security blanket. It did not help. He did not sleep the rest of the night.

Over the next few weeks, the dreams haunted him increasingly during the days and he would often experience them as he gave a customer change at the register or as he calculated taxes in his back office. Soon, the visions were coming so fast and frequently, that Logan grew increasingly worried about his mental state.

"Honey, I think I need to start seeing a psychiatrist about these dreams and visions I've been having lately. I can no longer go an hour, sometimes a half-hour, without one. Sometimes I fall asleep in my office chair and find myself on the bridge of a starship. Sometimes I'll have a vision while serving a customer and in the middle of a sentence I will become transfixed and wake a minute or two later with the customer staring at me and calling my name to wake me up. What's wrong with me?"

Early one evening, as he was totaling the day's receipts after closing time, Logan raised his head briefly to stretch his neck muscles, when his eyes fell upon a photo of Hannah from when they had taken a ten-day cruise through the Gulf of Mexico. Staring at her in her sun-dress and sunglasses, Logan drifted off into a reverie to find himself in the recreation room of the Venture chatting up the lieutenant from the administration division with whom he was playing table tennis and who could have been Hannah's twin. The top button of her uniform had come free without her knowledge, exposing the top inch or so of her cleavage. Logan could hardly take his eyes off it, and was debating with himself whether he should mention it before someone else did or should he just enjoy the view for as long as he could. "Of course," he thought in his dream, "maybe she knows it and is just waiting to see if I am gentleman enough to tell her."

When he awoke back in the hardware store, he tried hard to recall her name, but couldn't. "What was her name?" he asked himself. "It was something like Anna, wasn't it?"

More and more frequently the dream of life on board the Venture seemed more real, more vivid, than life in the small

town of Danville, Kentucky. In fact, Logan seemed to remember more of his life on board Venture that of his life in
Danville, so much so that he began to debate within himself
as to which was the reality of his existence.

#

Kekla sensed that time in Logan's mind seemed longer
than it was. That was good. That generated a psychological
inertia; the longer Logan believed he was in a pleasant place,
the less likely he was to want to leave it.

Kekla increased the dosage a little more, being careful to
inject enough to keep Logan peaceful, but not enough to give
him night terrors that would cause him to struggle violently
and possibly awaken to the truth.

#

For a while, the visions and dreams of being an astronaut
stopped. Logan's life without them felt empty, dull, boring,
insipid. No matter how many times he played Frisbee with
his grandchildren and his golden Labrador, no matter how
many times he and Hannah planned their retirement together
after making love, at night he would always find himself
standing in the backyard, gazing at the stars, wondering what
life was like on other planets.

The dream and visions began to return, in small, vague
excerpts at first, then developing into long, detailed adven-
tures spanning constellations; he reveled in camaraderie
among the ships' crews; in wild, hedonistic port calls on dis-

tant worlds; and in intrigue and mystery as his ship approached a new world and he rounded up a team to explore its surface.

The dreams and visions were no longer hindrances to his life. They were his life. He waited for them. They gave his life a satisfaction he could never know in a small, out of the way, backwater of life. He sought ways to induce them. Sometimes he would sit for hours in his office chair, eyes closed, concentrating all his energy on bringing them out of his subconscious. Finally, they began to return with greater and greater strength.

Now his dreams were more lucid than ever. He could hear the loudspeaker system as the Captain called him to the office. Logan suspected that the Captain was going to ask him to lead a team to explore Stheno D, which he was eager to do.

#

Kekla pushed out more hallucinogen.

#

Logan was standing before the altar with Hannah while their pastor pronounced them man and wife. At the wedding reception, their friends toasted them. Beer, bourbon, and champagne seemed to flow endlessly, while a bluegrass band played and everyone danced. In their hotel at Cumberland Falls, Logan and Hannah tore off each other's clothes to make love until the sun rose over the hills and the black velvet of night faded into a warm gold masking the stars.

"Stars like Algol," Logan thought as he stood at the window peering out at the night sky while Hannah slumbered, her long, blonde tresses partially covering her breasts and the mingling of their bodies' chemistry creating their first son. He smiled and felt a warm glow of happiness settle over his being.

Yet, no matter how hard he struggled to forget the visions and focus on his life ahead, he could not erase the stars from his mind.

"Algol," he thought as he peered out the window. "is the brightest star in the constellation Perseus. The name is Arabic and means 'the ghoul'. Algol is a trinary system with each star named unofficially after one of the three gorgons of Greek mythology: Medusa, Euryale, and Stheno. Stheno was the most vicious of the three, having killed more men than her other two sisters combined."

How did he know all that, he asked himself. A hardware store owner shouldn't know stuff like that.

Logan stepped out of the room into the summer morning and searched the skies for the fading constellation of Perseus. Finally, he saw Algol high in the sky, dangling in the night like the opal earring of that blonde lieutenant in his dreams with whom he had finally slept after weeks of pursuit. What was her name? It began with an H. God, that had been a night! Her love-making had drained him until he could barely stand. He remembered her loving more vividly than he could remember Hannah's, which was only a few minutes ago. He had mentioned something about a planet around Algol to the lieutenant, but the memory was hazy.

Algol again. What was it that he remembered about Algol? There was something he wanted to know about Algol.

As he stood and stared at the star, he closed his tired eyes for only a moment to rest them, but he soon found himself about to enter the Captain's office on the Venture.

Logan straightened his uniform and knocked on the Captain's door. Through the door he heard Captain Phelps say, "Enter."

Logan opened the door and walked smartly over to the Captain at his desk and came to attention. "Lieutenant Rickover reporting as ordered, sir."

Captain Phelps looked up somberly and asked, "Lieutenant, I have heard that you carry an illegal weapon with you on missions. Is that true?"

Logan felt the sweat break on his brow. This was unexpected; Logan had hoped that he was called to the Captain's office to receive an assignment. Now it appeared he might have been called to be punished. Unauthorized weapons were a serious offense and Logan was guilty. "Yes, sir."

"What kind is it?"

"An old-style pocket knife with a three-inch blade, sir."

"Why do you carry it?"

"It's reliable and very utilitarian, sir. It has minimal moving parts. If all else fails, I have it, sir. Also, it's something of a family heirloom. I inherited it from my father, who inherited it from his father, and so on for several generations."

"That's what I like about you, Lieutenant. You're pragmatic. That's why I want you for this mission. As you know we are orbiting Stheno D. What do you know about it?"

Logan sighed in relief. "Stheno D is the only planet in the

system to have climatic conditions humans can reasonably tolerate. It is about the size of Earth and has approximately the same gravity, but is warmer and wetter, causing most of the planet to be tropical, but its equatorial region is so dense that some exobotanists classify it as hypertropical. No signs of a civilization have yet been detected, though a very primitive culture like our early Stone Age may exist. Stheno D's colonization is critical to human expansion in the area, given the lack of water for several light years in any direction and its abundance here, making it something of an oasis. All twenty-six personnel sent to its surface in the nine years since humans first landed on it have disappeared, a higher casualty rate than for all the other star systems being explored. This has resulted in no flora or fauna having yet been collected from it."

"Have any of those personnel been found?"

"No, sir. No reason has been found for their disappearance either despite intensive intelligence collection by shipboard systems on previous missions to this system, primarily due to the dense jungle canopy, which degrades or inhibits sensor performance for reasons yet to be determined."

"Correct," said Captain Phelps. "And I am willing to wager that you have already surmised what your role in our mission is to be."

Logan struggled to suppress a growing smile. "I believe it will be to lead a team to the surface to find out why the canopy inhibits sensors."

"Partly. I want you to take a team down into their equatorial region for one of the planet's days, which is about seventy-five hours." The captain brought up a map of the planet's surface on the large viewing screen in front of his desk. Several spots in the equatorial region were flagged. "Here are the best clearings where you can land. Pick the one you think best. Record everything that happens in your vicinity for a full day, transmitting all data back as it occurs. You and your crew will note down your observations and transmit those every six hours. Take ladders, ropes, and any other gear you will need to climb to the canopy and collect samples. You can take anyone from the crew you like, but no more than twelve. Stay in the clearing you choose as much as possible. We can monitor you there and send a back-up team in case of an emergency. You will also choose the composition of the back-up team. Is that understood?"

"Yes, sir."

Logan examined the marked clearings closely and enlarged the view of one. He focused on it intensely. "We'll land at this one. It's on a hill just to the west of a tall mountain like a church steeple. If, for some reason, someone strays from the ship, he'll be able to navigate back, even if his comms are out. Also, any line-of-sight communications will reach a little farther. It also seems to have less vegetation that might interfere with the landing."

The captain smiled. "Good thinking. Do you have any questions?"

"Yes, sir. Normally, a mission like this is planned weeks in advance and I know that we came with three probes specifically designed to examine the canopy—"

"We have already lost the three probes. The last disappeared beneath the canopy seventy-two hours ago and has not been heard from since. I will not go back to Admiral

Wolterman to tell him I failed in my mission. I am taking something back. Any other questions?"

"No, sir."

"Be ready to go when dawn reaches that clearing, which, I believe, is in six hours. I wish you the best of luck. I know you'll do well."

"Thank you, sir." Logan came to attention, and then turned and exited as smartly as he had entered, but with a smile he did not have before.

Once in the passageway, as was his habit, he drew the knife from his trousers pocket and began flicking it open with one hand. Since Logan's father had passed down the knife from his dad, Logan had continuously toyed with it, trying to find a way to open it with one hand. After several months, he succeeded. He found he could place his thumb against the top edge of the blade and open it a little, and then flick his wrist to snap it to full extension. Now, he could open it so quickly and smoothly that his shipmates thought he owned a switchblade. Logan stepped rapidly down the passageway, feeling as if he were dancing on air and flicking his knife open and closed, open and closed. Leading a reconnaissance team down to an unexplored and dangerous planet would be a terrific bullet for his evaluation and would almost ensure his promotion to lieutenant commander.

He stopped at a door and knocked. The blonde lieutenant opened it. She was in a bathrobe, having just showered. He kissed her and told her the good news. She looked frightened and told him to be careful. He assured her he would. They hugged, and then kissed, and then kissed more passionately. Then Logan entered the room and closed the door. They made love for an hour before Logan left reluctantly to continue with his assignment.

Soon, Logan found himself on the planet known as Stheno D. He remembered landing in the ship's launch along with twelve other crew members. He could feel the growing pull of gravity as they descended through the atmosphere and vibration of the sub-light engines as they ramped down on landing. The Venture's sensors had confirmed prior to departure that the planet's temperature was suitable for humans and the atmosphere had the right mix to support human life. Instead of their heavier, bulkier spacesuits which protected against any environmental hazard, Logan opted for the regular field uniforms. The Venture's sensor arrays and drones had not detected anything similar to harmful plant life, animals, or gases known in other systems, making the spacesuits overkill for protection from the environment, but also the field uniforms made running much easier and faster, should the team have to run from something. Logan left the team's medic, petty officer first class Worth, in the ship to monitor the launch's sensors for possible threats and to be ready to provide first aid should anyone be injured by wildlife or venomous plants.

Even though they planned on going less than a hundred meters from the ship, Logan ensured everyone carried a PI-C290 communications band, which strapped to the wrist and gave range and bearing to the ship from the wearer's location as well as providing interpersonal communications, and a Hawking S-550 black particle sidearm with two power packs. Logan divided up the rest of the crew, including himself, into six pairs, which set about placing cameras and mini-sensors one hundred meters out from the ship at every sixty degrees around the launch.

Leaving petty officer Worth in the ship now reduced the team to set up the personnel to set up the sensors to eleven, therefore Logan paired up with a third class petty officer named Franks. Franks had always impressed Logan as a competent, quick-thinking crewman, though he had a few harmless personal quirks that had somehow earned him the moniker "Quark". Logan didn't understand it, but those of the most recent classes of personnel just out of basic training found it hysterical.

Just as the team finished setting up their sensor array, Franks said he needed to take a crap urgently, but he didn't want to do so in the open with the female crewmembers around and he didn't think he could make it back to the ship in time. "I shouldn't have had that god-awful, imitation sauer kraut for breakfast," he said.

At the edge of the jungle, Logan said, "Go behind that tree," while nodding toward a tree that resembled a tall palm. "I'll watch for wildlife."

Logan followed Franks to the tree and stayed on the side nearest the ship, while Franks went to the other. While he waited, watching in all directions, Logan noticed something about the mountain: about halfway up on the southern side protruded two large, round masses of rock that resembled breasts. Logan smiled.

Franks was taking longer than expected and Logan was becoming impatient as well as curious about what lay beyond the tree line. Stepping a few meters from Franks, Logan found an animal path through the brush and tall ferns. Tracks running down it seemed to be those of a huge insect. They seemed fresh and Logan wondered if he could catch a glimpse of the creature. Just then Franks called out, "Okay, Lieutenant, I'm finished."

"Yeah, great, congratulations," muttered Logan. Then he called out, "Wait right there. I've found some tracks and I want to see if the life form is still around."

Logan drew his sidearm in case of the unexpected made sure it was already set to half-strength, which would stun most creatures, but would not kill them. Logan knew to leave the sight of one's ship in unfamiliar terrain was not good practice, but he was eager to to find the first animal on this planet and name it for himself as was fleet tradition. He also did not want to bring an inexperienced crewman into the forest.

"Franks, stay where you are and where the rest of the crew can see you too. I'll keep talking so you know where I am. He took several steps. "Now I'm twenty meters from you." He saw nothing and so took several more. "Now, I'm thirty meters from you." He called out again at forty and fifty meters. At sixty meters he decided to give up and go back. "Sixty meters and I'm coming back."

After a few steps, he heard something rustle the bushes to his right, and then all around. He aimed his sidearm at the last bush that rustled, but something rushed out, knocking the sidearm from his hand before all went black. He remembered being dragged along the path and the feeling of the forest duff on his back, the strange smell of alien flowers, and what seemed to be the chirping of large insects. It seemed so real. Then he realized it was real.

The revelation hit with tremendous power. All the illusions and the vague sensations fell away. Logan had no wife. Hannah was the name of the blonde lieutenant, but in his mind, she was his wife. The only times he had been to Kentucky was to visit his grandfather, who had owned a hardware store in Danville. He had always found his grandfather's stories about living in Danville boring, when he was young, but in later years he found they gave him feelings of peace and tranquility in difficult times, because they described an idyllic existence Logan knew he would never see. Somehow, the memories of his grandfather's stories, his own memories of Danville, and his own life had become not just intertwined, but had been blended together, so that Logan could not distinguish where his grandfather's stories ended and his own life began. It was becoming very clear now.

As he opened his eyes, the back of Logan's head throbbed with a great, dull pain as did a spot in the center of his back to the left of his spine and continuing to his stomach. Something that felt like steel bars wrapped around him tightly, preventing all but the smallest movements of his arms and no movement of his legs and held him against what felt like a firm mattress. He heard a sound like breathing that seemed to be coming from all directions. The air was hot, humid, and musty. Logan was sweating profusely. A series of sharp pains clustered near his stomach. With some effort, he was able to move a hand to the spot and feel four hard bumps the size of tennis balls buried under his skin. One of them moved as if something inside it was stirring. Then another moved. "My God," he thought, "these are eggs." A mixture of sickening fear and revulsion shot through him.

Logan opened his eyes and saw what appeared to be a smooth, stone wall glowing bright green. "Bioluminescent fungus," he thought. To the right the fungus lined a tunnel disappearing into the darkness. To the left the tunnel extended maybe seventy-five meters and then opened into the jungle where he saw daylight, trees, and ferns. He looked at the bars binding him. They looked like insect legs. He glanced around. The legs were holding him against the underside of a gigantic insect-like creature. Logan craned his head despite the increasing pain as something like a flexible tube stuck in the back of his head resisted. After he had moved his head as far as possible, Logan could see a large, cockroach-like head, but with a dozen unblinking, arachnid eyes looking down at him. It said something to him in what was clearly a language, but one he did not speak. He yelled and began to fight furiously against Kekla, who had just told him that to resist was useless and that giving in to the dreams would make his last few hours as pleasant as possible.

#

Kekla increased the strength of the hallucinogen to the maximum.

#

For an instant, Logan flashed back to lying in Hannah's arms. He felt peaceful and quiet and wanting to drift off to sleep, but slowly Hannah's arms turned into cold, armor-plated legs and her gentle snoring became the terrifying click of mandibles gnashing together furiously. Logan opened his eyes and found himself still wrapped in Kekla's horrible embrace.

Logan struggled fiercely for several minutes, but then he saw that struggling was not only in vain, but it was also a waste of energy: the legs had not budged. He took a few deep breaths to calm himself so he could gather his thoughts. He examined the legs more closely to see if they had a weak point. He found one. Where the legs bent around Logan's body was, naturally, a joint in each. Each joint was made of soft flesh and tendons and was slightly in front of Logan's arms.

Logan worked his right hand back down his side and into his pocket, where he kept his knife. He pulled it slowly out of his pocket and worked its way up his body to in front of his heart and to the left. Once he managed to get his hand free and between the legs, Logan opened the blade with a quick flick of the wrist, and quickly cut through the tendons of the top leg. The leg flopped away and Kekla let out a penetrating, high-pitched squeal of pain. Logan used the sudden freedom of this hand to cut the tendons of the second leg and his captor squealed again. The two right legs clutched Logan more tightly around his trunk, but Logan had managed to get both arms free. A motion above caught Logan's attention and he glanced up. Kekla was looking down and shrieking with its mouth wide open revealing showing four large fangs. It dipped its head suddenly to bite, but Logan thrust the knife straight up into the roof of Kekla's mouth, pulled it out, and swiped behind his head to sever the tube feeding into his brain. Kekla fell over, its mandibles clicking rapidly, its two working legs flexing inward almost crushing Logan as they fell, but just as they hit the ground, Logan squirmed free of Kekla's limbs and the tube feeding him nutrients went limp and slipped out. Logan yanked out the remaining part of the hallucinogen tube from his head and rolled over the tunnel's floor and stopped on his stomach. Kekla was twitching furiously and thrashing about. Logan sprang up and scanned the area. Another of Kekla's species was charging at him with its mouth open. Logan snatched a large stone from the tunnel floor and flung it, striking the alien between the eyes. It flopped to the ground, twisting and squealing madly. Logan leapt forward and stabbed it twice between the eyes, silencing it.

From the darkness down the tunnel, Logan heard the chirping of dozens more of creatures like Kekla and the clicking of what seemed to be dozens of legs covered by hard shell moving in his direction. More of the creatures were coming for him. Logan ran to the tunnel's mouth and out into the jungle, the bright daylight almost blinding him as he emerged.

Logan found a path outside the cave mouth and sprinted down it and through the jungle. He had no idea where he was. He glanced at his wrist. He was still wearing his communications band. He tried calling the ship while he ran, but no one responded. Whatever was in the jungle canopy that blocked the ship's sensors, must have been blocking the comm band's transmissions, including the automatic transmissions that reported his position every minute. He glanced around and through a gap in the canopy ahead spotted the steeple-like mountain near the ship and its prominent breasts. He knew he was west of the mountain. The ship was between him and the mountain. He picked up his pace. He ran until his mouth felt full of copper and his side felt as if someone had jabbed a knife into it. He pushed past the pain and kept running.

Just as he was about to collapse, Logan spotted a four-man reconnaissance team with sidearms at the ready about fifty meters ahead. He realized they were a search team. Logan tried to yell a warning, but could only croak out a loud whisper, "Run! Run! Go back!"

The team ran up to him. Two, one of which was Franks, ran a few meters down the trail to ward off any pursuers, the other two put their arms around Logan's shoulders to support him. "Good Lord, Lieutenant, where have you been?" said Franks. "We've been searching for you for a week."

Then Franks and his shipmate saw the bushes on either side of the trail a quarter kilometer back along the path to Kekla's lair rustle violently. Franks called out, "The jungle's moving 250 meters back."

Logan knew Kekla's siblings were coming. "Get everyone back to the ship. Make ready to launch," he said, trying to catch his breath. One of the men blocking the path called on his comm unit and told the rest of the crew they had located Lieutenant Rickover and they were to return to the ship and prepare to launch.

The team ran back to the ship as fast as they could while supporting Logan, who continued to croak out, "For God's sake, run! Run!" Soon, they were running into the clearing surrounding the landing site. Logan scanned back along the trail to see if anything was following. He saw the bushes shaking about fifty meters back and guessed it was Kekla's kindred, but could not be certain. He did not like not knowing exactly where the enemy was.

As they entered the clearing, Logan saw another transport alongside the first. A few personnel were scattered about, but they came running to help when they saw the team returning with Logan.

Logan saw that some of his original crew were gathered at the ramp to the ship's door. They all turned to him, mouths agape at seeing him alive, as he broke free from his shipmates' supporting arms, ran gasping up the ramp, through the launch, and to petty officer Worth, who stood at the medical locker near the pilot's chair counting bandages. Logan yelled, "Doc! Get your scalpel! Get these things out of me! Cut'em out of me! They're hatching! Oh, God! Do something!"

Logan's shout startled Worth, who spun around and shrank back in horror at the sight of something behind Logan. Logan glanced back.

Five of Kekla's siblings were scuttling into the crew compartment and racing toward Logan and Worth. Logan sprang to the pilot's chair and hit the general quarters alarm, which was automatically transmitted to the Venture. A back-up team would be on scene fully-armed in a few minutes. From the ship's door came screaming and the sounds of sidearms being fired. Before Logan could grab something for a weapon, the lead Sthenan had grabbed his ankles and was dragging him out of the ship. As he went out the ship's airlock, he could see the area was swarmed by Sthenans carrying off his shipmates.

Once back in the cave, the Sthenan slung Logan, bleeding and bruised from the brutal journey back, into the middle of the floor. Logan landed roughly and rolled, choking on the cloud of dust that arose from his impact. He raised his head and looked around. Sthenans were dragging in the crew, who were struggling, kicking, and screaming to no avail. A few were already caught in the alien embrace, begging for mercy while the ovipositors and hallucinogen tubes were being inserted. Franks had already been subdued and was standing expressionless, while the alien behind him snuggled up and wrapped its cold, steel-like legs around him tightly.

Logan glanced behind him and jerked back in terror. Standing over him was Kekla, four limp legs dangling, tendons severed, a white fluid Logan assumed to be blood draining from its mouth. Its mandibles clicked as it stared at Logan on the floor and once again it spoke in its unintelligible language. Logan had no idea as to what Kekla was saying, but judging by its rapid delivery and intense tone, he guessed he was being cursed.

Logan buckled over in sudden, intense pain and screamed as Kekla's mandibles continued clicking with increasing fury, not in anger, but in unbounded delight, as it waited eager to see its young, blood-drenched and sated, emerge from Logan's pale corpse.

Logan's last thought as the back-up team entered, firing their particle weapons, was to wish he that he was in Danville, with Hannah sleeping on his shoulder, her long hair brushing lightly against his face in a tickling, golden wave.

12

Murder by Plastic

When Alan Patterson awoke, he found himself naked and bound with wire to a heavy wooden chair with duct tape sealing his mouth. His head throbbed. The night was hot and humid and sweat rolled down his forehead and into his eyes, blurring his vision. He blinked a few times to clear them. He noticed a large, sharply dressed man sitting on another wooden chair a few feet away. The man seemed very serious and squinted through small, piggish eyes.

Glancing around, Alan saw that he was in a dilapidated warehouse. A half dozen younger, just-as-sharply dressed, just-as-serious men stood behind the seated man. One held a bucket of water. On a small work-bench to his left, Alan saw a hacksaw, a blowtorch, pliers, a claw hammer, a skinning knife, and a meat cleaver. He also saw a dozen stolen credit cards he had recently bought from Joey "Snake Eyes" Abandonato and had intended to sell.

The large man reached inside his suit and pulled out a driver's license. He scrutinized it and then looked at Alan's face for several seconds. "This is a crappy photo of you, Mr.

Wilson," he muttered. He tossed the license onto the floor. "You may not know my face, but you know who I am. I am Don Antonio Vespucci. I live down the street from you." The Don gritted his teeth and clenched his fists as his entire body seemed to tense. He shifted in his chair and then, apparently trying to relax enough to speak, took a deep breath and exhaled slowly. "I'm the father of the boy you ran down while speeding through our neighborhood three weeks ago."

Alan's eyes widened and he shook his head violently while trying to shout through the duct tape. *"No! I didn't do it! I'm not Steve Wilson!"*

The Don raised his voice, drowning out Alan's muffled protests. "I can't begin to describe what you did to my family. No one should go through the agony of having a son die in his arms! Do you know what it's like to get a phone call telling you your child is in critical care? Your entire world collapses in a heartbeat!" Don Vespucci slammed his fists onto the arms of his chair. Then he seemed lost in thought while he adjusted his tie and fought back tears. "Isn't it strange how lives can change in an instant? The critical moment in my son's death lasted less than a second. He ran into the street to get his baseball just as his mom turned her back to say hello to Joey there and his wife Maria." He nodded to indicate the man to Alan's extreme left.

Alan turned his head as far as possible and looked into the cold, reptilian stare that had earned Joey his moniker. *"Joey?"* Alan tried to say under the tape. *"No! Forgive me, Joey! Forgive me!"*

The Don continued. "When Joey saw my son run into the

street, he glanced up just in time to see you speed over my Tony Jr. He recognized your car, your rear license, and the back of your head!"

Alan wept as he tried to shout from under the tape, *"Joey, forgive me! Tell him I was in Jersey then!"*

Again, the Don paused to calm down and assume a more professional tone. "Normally," said Don Vespucci, "I try to meet all the new people in our neighborhood as soon as someone moves in. Unfortunately, I've been busier than usual lately and haven't had time to visit anyone. Had I been able to introduce myself to you and had stressed, as I normally do, the value of family in my life and how I like things done in my neighborhood, perhaps we wouldn't be here."

Tears streamed from Alan's eyes and he shook. *"Please, take the tape off!"* came out only as "MnnmMnNmMnmMm."

"We might not have come to this regrettable situation if you hadn't decided to scurry out of town like a cockroach when you found out whose son you had just killed. It disgusts me that you abandoned your family to save your life! You're fortunate that I have principles so I don't hurt anyone's family. At this point, I have more respect for the rats that'll feed on your eyes than I do for you. Had you come to me after the accident and accepted responsibility, I might actually have had some admiration for you. I still would've killed you, but I would've killed you quickly."

Alan began to shake his head again as his eyes bulged from their sockets as he tried to scream *"I just stole Wilson's identity!"* through the duct tape.

"Don't waste the few breaths you have left. If I wanted

to hear your lies, I'd have Joey take the tape off." The Don breathed deeply through his nose and exhaled as if he were trying to relax. Anger rose in his voice. "What kind of idiot runs to Brooklyn where we can just snatch him off the street? You should have at least left the state." Don Vespucci stretched out a hand toward Joey. "Gimme the hammer. We're going to start with the foot that was on the gas and work our way up. Pete, keep the water handy. We don't want Mr. Wilson to pass out from the pain."

Alan struggled against the duct tape and again tried in vain to scream through the tape, *"I'm not Steve Wilson! I bought his credit cards from Joey just two weeks ago!"*

As he watched Joey smirk as he handed a hammer to the Don, Alan remembered his last night with Maria at Noel's Motel and began to weep. As she pulled on her clothes, she warned him: "Joey's smarter than you think. It wouldn't surprise me if he knows about us already. He has ears everywhere. Me, he'll just beat, but you—well, just don't let him find out."

13

Alain Devereux Falls in Love

Late one evening, Alain Devereux is lying naked in bed with his head propped up on his pillows and plays with an inflatable sex doll, examining it closely, bouncing it upon his lap as if it were a child, holding it above him, now and then teasing it by bringing its lips close to his as if about to kiss it passionately and then pushing it away suddenly with a cruel laugh. He speaks to it.

"I loved you from the moment I first saw you. What a *strange* feeling that was! I had never thought it possible that given my taste for elegant women, long and cool with a certain grace and a certain *hauteur* attitude, a bold over-confidence in their stride, and a feline suppleness to their movements, that I should be so thunderstruck by an average woman of slightly better than average looks that I happened to spot in such a run of the mill place as the vegetable section of a small town supermarket. I could not take my eyes off you. There was a certain inexpressible, sensual movement in your hips, a certain barely perceptible sway to your breasts, and a lusciousness in your lips that aroused me in ways I cannot explain. I suspected that you had noticed me watching from the way you occasionally glanced over your shoulder as if to double-check some item but then smiled. No one smiles at turnips or broccoli or lettuce. After you did that a few times, I started noticing the subtle movement of your large, beautiful eyes as they quickly gave me the "once over" not once, but several times over the next few minutes. I sensed that I had an opportunity for an unspoken conversation with erotic undertones when you started for the cucumbers. I saw a chance for a scene like that in *Animal House*, yet on a much subtler, more mature level that I suspected you would appreciate. Coming up with an icebreaker was a challenge for me, because I wanted to stimulate a response from you, yet do it in such a way that was not crude, but that gave you the chance to drop the hint of your choice. When you picked up a cucumber, all that came to mind was to ask if you had seen any good ones. For a second, I was afraid that I had scared you off, but that coquettish look you gave me and the slight giggle spoke volumes. I was very pleasantly surprised at how easily you chatted up and agreed to dinner and a movie.

"I hated your reaction the next morning though, as I was dressing at your place and something about sorcery was on the History Channel...when I told you in a moment of straightforward, blunt honesty that surprised even myself that I am a sorcerer and my overriding passion in life is black magic. It wasn't the confused look of shock as if you were trying to decide if I were thoroughly crazy or thoroughly evil or even the way you courteously and respectfully told me to get out and not come back that hurt and offended me. It was the contempt in those beautiful eyes that had undressed me over dinner and the scorn in your normally melodic voice that drove red-hot nails into my heart and bones. I can never forgive those things you said to deliberately hurt me, obviously trying to ensure that I would never return, when I had dreamed of sharing with you some of the greatest pleasures I have ever known. I had envisioned so much for us and now all those hopes were cruelly shattered and lay at my feet like so much nauseating garbage.

"For these reasons, when you turned to fetch my jacket, I stole a hairbrush, a photo, and your stockings to use in casting a spell so that I could always have you and you would always be with me and you would always be mine to do with as I please. I had your body for a night; now I'll have your soul forever."

"Let me out of this, Alain!" says the doll. "Let me out! I promise to love you forever. I promise! Please let me out." The doll begins to sob. "I promise never to leave you. I will live with you and I swear I will be happy forever. Just please return me to human form, Alain. Please. Please! Alain! Alain!"

Alain laughed with a sardonic crescendo rising from the infernal depths within his mind.

14

Necromancers

To strengthen his powers, Alain Devereux had lain meditating in the grave clothes and coffin of his former master, Karl Sprenger, in the operating room of the abandoned St. Ursula Psychiatric Hospital for three days and nights. His only nourishment had been six ounces of a broth made from Sprenger's heart and brain taken every six hours. The occasional centipede crawling across his face or rat sniffing his fingers did not bother him. Instead, it tested his ability to focus his mind on conjuring his former master's spirit out of hell to reveal the one secret he had kept from his apprentice.

Alain switched on a flashlight. He raised the lid until it rested on the table supporting the coffin. He examined the two circles of priest's ashes surrounding the coffin and the smaller circle six feet away from those, in which Karl would appear, to ensure none had been broken by rats wandering through the room. Their continuity and the spells written in and around them in blood on the walls, floor, and ceiling, were the only things protecting him from Karl's power.

Movement in the hall beyond the entrance caught Alain's

eye. He watched and listened intently, but detected nothing more. He assumed it to be a rat and relaxed.

Alain took six dark red candles from a briefcase outside the coffin, lit them, and set them on the table. Once he was certain all was as it should be, Alain reached over, grasped the lid, and closed it as he lay back into the coffin. When it was nearly to, he turned off the flashlight and propped the coffin lid open with it. He began his final chant. When he finished, in a loud, commanding tone, he ordered the unholy powers of the underworld to bring forth Karl Sprenger.

When Alain opened his eyes, he saw his old mentor, naked and covered with the scars and stench of hell, crouching in the smaller circle designed to be his cell.

At first, Karl appeared confused. Then he recognized the room as the place where he taught Alain the basics of communicating with the dead. Seeing Alain hiding in the coffin, he laughed.

"You are exactly as I imagined you would be. You look like a mouse trying to hide in a jewelry box," said Karl. "My coffin is a nice touch, but it doesn't really help protect you. What do you want, Alain?"

"I want to know the secret you withheld from me. You used to hint at its nature, but never went into details. I want to surpass your skills. I know I can be better and more powerful than you ever were. I will be greater than you, the master necromancer and magus, but to do that, I must first know everything you know."

Karl tried to suppress a growing smile, but failed. "What do I get in return?"

"The more you tell me, the longer you stay out of hell."

"I commend you on an ingenious plan: if you can't get what you want from the master when he is alive, poison him, and conjure him up from the dead when he has to submit. I suspected that's what you were up to a few minutes after I awoke among the damned. Too bad you didn't learn to conceal your guilt as well as your plan. Strychnine in my coffee? You should have known I would recognize the symptoms easily. How many people have you seen me poison with strychnine? You should have at least been original. Tsk. Tsk. I would have served you better as a friend than as an enemy."

"Why would I try to conceal anything from you? What could the dead possibly do to the living? Haunt me? You taught me the spells to counter that. I will bring you back whenever I want and I will do to you whatever I want, because now I'm in control."

"Control? Really? There is a reason I am the master and you are the apprentice."

"You *were* the master; I *was* the apprentice. Now tell me what I want to know or I'll let you burn in hell for a few months more before summoning you again."

"As you wish." Karl smiled once again, but this time with an intensity in his eyes that revealed a burning hatred. "Communicating with the dead is useful only when one is alive, a very short time compared to how long one is dead. Therefore, the wise necromancer prepares for death by studying how to communicate with the living once he is dead."

"Intriguing. How do I do that?"

"How else? Raise spirits that appear of their own free will, ghosts known to haunt a certain location for example, and ask them how they communicate with the living. Once you know their ways, and there are many, you can communicate with whatever spirit you want, whenever you want."

"Fascinating. Have you communicated with anyone since you died?"

"Yes, of course. I have been in touch with Jack Thurston."

"Jack Thurston, the sorcerer that lives here in Santa Fe?"

"Yes, that's him. I have even struck a bargain with him: that I would teach him the ways of necromancy in exchange for a favor."

"What favor?"

"Following you."

Jack Thurston bolted from the entrance behind the coffin, knocked the flashlight from under the lid, slammed the lid shut, and quickly wrapped a chain around it, fastening it with a padlock. As Alain pleaded for his life, Jack fetched a can of gasoline from the hall, dowsed the coffin, and lit it with a match.

As the flames shot up, Alain choked on smoke and tried to bust out of the coffin while Karl laughed. As Alain screamed as the flames grew, Karl shouted, "Get used to it! I have a lot more to teach you once you arrive in hell!"

15

Love for a Stunning Woman

She was a stunning woman, delicate, graceful, eloquent, with an insightful, analytical mind. She loved rarely, but when she did, she loved powerfully. Her only flaw was in loving me, lowering herself to grace me with her presence, a self-demeaning act I could neither comprehend nor stomach. For this reason, I rid myself of her—ruining a damned fine chainsaw in the process.

16

Special

I told my psychiatrist that last week I discovered creatures inside my head that keep shuffling about, fighting, screaming, and telling me to do horrendous things. He wouldn't let me prove my point by using my pocketknife to peel back my scalp. He just grabbed my wrists and kept saying the creatures are imaginary. He was just jealous that they chose me and no one else to enlighten. After all, I couldn't find any in his head or any of the others in the random sampling I took while walking back home that day. I feel kind of special now.

Phil Slattery is a native of Kentucky but has traveled widely. He has a B.A. in German and Russian from Eastern Kentucky University. He started writing poetry while in the Navy during the late 1980's. Most of these have been collected into *Nocturne: Poems of Love, Distance, and the Night, a callous and disinterested lover.* Over time he has turned to fiction, mostly dark, and intends to take up writing full time after he retires. He has also published another collection of short stories with Amazon, *The Scent and Other Stories,* and a novelette, *Click.* His website is phils-lattery.wordpress.com. He also has an Amazon author's page at amazon.com/author/philslattery. He can be found on Facebook (www.facebook.com /slatterysartofhorror), Twitter (@philslattery201), and various other social media. Some of his fiction, poetry, and photography as well as interviews can be found scattered about on the Internet.

Also by Phil Slattery

Click

Frank Martinez, a policeman with the Corpus Christi Police Department, has unintentionally shot and killed an unarmed man when called to intercede in a domestic violence case. To recover from the guilt while the incident is under investigation by the CCPD, Frank's fiancée arranges for him to stay on a secluded island owned by her father's former law partner. While dozing one night on a lounge chair in the yard, he awakes to find two hit men slipping onto the island and breaking into the cabin. Are they after him? Are they after the cabin's owner? Most importantly, how is he going to reach his pistol in his luggage in the bedroom? Readers' comments include:

"Author has a wonderful ability to develop the characters using few words. Great foreshadowing to build suspense. And then a really outstanding twist at the end that left me smiling."

"A lot of detail goes into both the psychological aspects of the story as well as the action. This one is packed with every character's motives, inner dialogue, and very well thought out. When it gets to the action it keeps this up as well as adding a lot of excitement."

"Smart, fast-paced, and full of action. The characters are well done and don't suffer from the usual boring tropes too much, and the two criminals are interesting as the author knows how to do 'bad guys' rather well."

"Author Phil Slattery takes us on an interesting ride. He gives a twist ending to the story, that once revealed, you realize he peppered the story with clues. The second twist ending hits out of left field, and left this reader wanting for more."

"The motivation is as old as storytelling, but that doesn't make it bad. Slattery's words make us care for the main character and seeing his view of his marriage leave us, in the end, feeling sad for him in his moment of triumph."

The Scent and Other Stories

In this collection of short stories, Phil Slattery explores the dark, sometimes violent, sometimes twisted, sometimes touching side of love, the side kept not only from public view, but sometimes from our mates. Set in the modern era, these stories range from regretting losing a lover to forbidden interracial love in the hills of 1970's Kentucky to a mother's deathbed confession in present-day New Mexico to debating pursuing a hateful man's wife to the callous manipulation of a lover in Texas. Praise for stories contained in "The Scent and Other Stories" includes:

"The Scent"

"This story has a lovely dreamy quality whilst being unsettling too. It lingers on half processed emotional experiences and leaves the reader asking 'what if' and 'if only' - feelings that are familiar for so many people."

"This descriptive piece about remembrance, the thought of what might have been, is a common sad thread that will resonate with those have experienced the pain of that one love lost. Slattery's use of scent was exquisite as we feel Quinn's pain and hope that he finds his peace, at last."

"Decision"

"Fantastic writing - I held my breath for most of the story. The descriptions of the countryside and the people were beautiful and the tension compelling. This could possibly be the start of a novel or a suite of stories. Thank you very much and good luck with your writing in the future"

"Suspenseful and engaging. The dialogue and descriptions kept pace with the action. Well done."

"A Good Man"

"Lots of detail examining an old question of how do you judge a person's life. It left me wondering."

"The Slightest of Indiscretions"

"Excellent writing brings this poignant story to life and makes the reader work to understand more of what might be. Very many thanks for a satisfying, emotionally intelligent read..."

Nocturne: Poems of Love, Distance, and the Night, a callous and disinterested Lover

Nocturne: Poems of Love, Distance, and the Night, a callous and disinterested lover is a collection of Phil Slattery's poetry written from the mid-80's to mid-90's, a turbulent, fluid time in his life in many ways, but especially romantically. He has taken many of the poems written (many of which were published in various magazines) during those years and compiled them into a dark narrative capturing the emotional turmoil of an anonymous narrator who descends from romantic love for a woman into a lonely world of alcohol and nightclubs, where his only love is the night that envelops him psychologically, emotionally, and physically. This is an emotional and psychological odyssey for the reader, exploring the bliss of love to the depths of despair and then to resignation to one's fate in an existential crisis. Readers' comments include:

"...All in all, Nocturne, is a beautiful but sad read that speaks to the reality of love and holds nothing back. It engages the mind and the heart longing for lasting, meaningful love that always seems just outside of its reach..."

"I like this author's poems which have a great feel to them. The book is about love but a lot more is included inside the pages... A few of the poems held descriptive words about nature and I enjoyed the way the picture author paints in the readers mind..."

"...The whole thing is sad emotionally and very bittersweet and left me feeling rather melancholy when I was finished. With both the poems and the introduction this is a very personal look at part of the author's life. He comes across as a very real and interesting person..."